Gumshoe

Published in Great Britain in 1998 by
Slow Dancer Press
59 Parliament Hill London NW3 2TB

Originally published by Fontana Books, 1971

British Library Cataloguing-in-Publication Data.
A catalogue record for this book is available from the British
Library.

ISBN   1 871033 44 6

Slow Dancer Fiction titles are available in the U.K. through
Turnaround Publisher Services and in the U.S.A. through
Dufour Editions inc.

Cover design: Keenan

Slow Dancer Logo: East Orange

Printed in Great Britain by The Guernsey Press Co. Ltd.

This book is set in Palatino 11/14

Slow Dancer Press

Gumshoe

Neville Smith

Slow Dancer Press

Why worry? Why be doubtful and confused?
Why be gnawed by suspicion? Consult cool
careful, confidential, discreet investigator.
George Anson Philips. Glenview 9521

The High Window
Raymond Chandler

For Maurice Hatton

INTRODUCTION

If I'm not mistaken, I met Neville Smith in the bar at Yorkshire television in late summer, 1968. He was working as an actor. When a mutual friend, Maurice Hatton, showed us his film *Praise Marx and Pass the Ammunition*, I think I said to Neville: "Why don't you write a thriller?"

He gave me a script of a haunting film he'd written (which Ken Loach had just made) about the death of a trades unionist, called *There's a Kind of Hush* – or *The Pope and Alan Ball*. He also gave me the opening pages of what would turn out to be *Gumshoe*. I don't think it then had a title. And I found I'd stumbled on a writer with the grace of Jackie Milburn and the wit of S.J.Perelman.

I had thought he was writing a thriller. In fact he was constructing a self-portrait; a record of what it was like to have been a teenager in the English provinces in the Fifties. "I want to write *The Maltese Falcon*; I want to record 'Blue Suede Shoes'." He could describe a life unlike my own yet one I would like to have lived. His world was warm, funny, observant, generous, ironic, scrupulous, complex.

For four months he brought in every day two or three hand-written pages which would make me laugh; I was the stenographer. At first there were just the two of us. Later Maurice took us off to a cottage to make us behave 'professionally', to turn what Neville had already written into a coherent script. He would lie on a sofa issuing instructions, discussing what Chandler or Hammett would 'do'; Neville would go in fury into the kitchen to write; what Neville wrote would be at the same time a counter-attack against Maurice - and magically funny. So we produced a script I took to Albert Finney, who was the first person I ever met who did impressions of Bogart. (Of course, Belmondo had impersonated Bogart in *A Bout De Souffle*.) Later, with Albert, we wrote another draft.

The making wasn't much fun. In those days the British film industry was still a hidebound business both in its practices and in its thinking. I doubt if more than a handful of people on the film knew what it was about, that within the framework of a pastiche of a film noir there lurked a human story. I guess that's why it's such an oddball of a film - fresh ideas within such a conventional framework.

But I've never lost any of my love or admiration

for Neville, who is in some ways, I think, the best writer I've ever come across. This book - the book of the film - I've never read. I couldn't bear it if I found a joke he hadn't thought of when he wrote the film.

Stephen Frears
London, 1998

CHAPTER ONE

He looked like the kind of guy your mother would like to marry your sister. If you had a mother. If you had a sister.

He wore a three-button Italian suit, a Billy Eckstine-style flex-roll, buttondown collar, a slim-jim tie. Neat, flat-cut hair topped the lot off. The perfect brother-in-law, circa 1957. He leaned back with his feet on the desk, bored out of his mind, looking at me sitting opposite in my vintage Grenfell trench coat (Hawkes of Savile Row, W.1. By Appointment); I wasn't bored.

I'd been making a pilgrimage to this guy's office every week for a year, only missing those occasions the dole people changed my days for signing on. The guy didn't mind. I should say 'man' really, not 'guy', because he's always chiding me for the way I speak, when he isn't trying to

11

copy it. You know what psychiatrists are, always trying to find a level on which to approach you. Always trying to show how like them you are. It's supposed to reassure you. It never works.

I ought to explain what I was doing there. My girl had married my brother and I'd gone hypochondriac badly. That isn't funny. My quack had recommended the shrink. It's all on the National Health, everyone can get it and a lot more should. If you feel you need it, apply now, because the way things are going, Heath and his gang might make it illegal. They're making it pretty hard now even if you're not a nutter, so jump in, it's not so bad. The theory is still 'care, from the cradle to the grave,' but the Cosa Nostra (Smith Square branch) are just hurrying the process along and making you pay a bomb for it. My name is Eddie Ginley.

"What are you thinking about?" he said.

"Nothing." I twiddled the *Echo*. "I'm thirty-one today."

"Happy birthday," he said.

"Thanks doc."

"How's the club?" He stretched and yawned.

"You really want to know?"

"Yeah. Sure."

"Great. I'm just doing the bingo calling at the moment, slip in a few gags here and there, I get to wear a tux. Tommy says he'll let me do a spot soon. He's weaning me in. That's what he says."

"Tommy's the boss?"

"Yeah."

He lapsed into silence again. I looked around the office I knew so well: his desk, his Grundig –

it's funny how psychiatrists like to have something German around them, even if, like mine, they're not analysts – his note-pad, the paintings on the wall done by children, the packed mantelpiece with his blood pressure machine, his dusty old stethoscope.

"Your turn."

"I can't think of anything to say," he said.

"What am I here for then?"

"I like you Eddie. It gets to this time in the week and I think, 'Great. Eddie's coming. We can have a laugh. Crack a few gags.' That's all really."

"Great. Meanwhile, head man, what about my cure?"

"What cure, Eddie?" He smiled and felt for his fags and as usual he wasn't carrying any, so I lobbed him my Luckies and Zippo.

"What cure?" came his voice again as he scrambled under his desk for the lighter. His face, red from exertion, peered over the edge of his blotter. "I told you when you started that you can't cure hypochondriasis. I just help you to live with it. Some great people were hypos – Darwin… er…" He struggled to think.

"Hitler?" I offered.

"Well, yes," he conceded, "but I was trying to offer encouragement."

"Elvis Presley."

"*Is* he?" The psych leaned across his desk with real interest, eyes widened as though I was giving him some real hot showbiz gossip.

"No. But it would really encourage me if he was."

"Oh!" He was really disappointed. He fell back in his chair and at last lit the Lucky. I had to prise the Zippo out of his grip as he gazed at the ceiling. I've lost three lighters to him that way, it must be part of the therapy.

He perked up again and leaned across his desk, eyes narrowing, fag drooping at the lip, "Listen, kid. You want some stuff? I can get you some real high grade scratch. No bum gear. For real. Shoot you up pretty good. You like, gringo?"

I started to laugh, he looked hurt.

"What was wrong with that?" he pleaded.

I stopped laughing, "Nothing. What's the film?"

He thought hard. "Well, no single film really. I mean, I can't remember any one particular character saying it, it's just the *genre*. You know."

I laughed again.

"Come on. What was wrong?"

"Nothing. Except scratch is – money, not dope. And as for gringo…" I shook my head. "Really, doc, you ought to pay more attention."

He got up and walked round the desk and sat on the edge of it looking down at me, "I try, Eddie, I really try. I watch old films on the telly and even write down bits to tell you. I can never remember them."

"You can always go back to medicine, doc."

He grinned down at me, "Okay, Eddie, I'll see you again next week."

"Right, doc." I stood, shrugged my trench coat back into place and made for the door.

"Actually," he began and I turned and looked at

14

him, "what I was attempting to say there was, do you need any pills?"

"Valium? Librium?"

He rolled back his top lip in what he thought was his best Bogart manner, leapt from his desk and adopted his Cagney stance. The voice was a mixture of the two. Or near enough.

"You… You just name your poison. Just name it kid. You dirty rat you!"

"Nah. I don't want anything. Even when I'm really low I only take them for a couple of days, then I forget and I always end up throwing them down the bog."

"Doesn't it help you?" he asked.

"Not me, doc, but it makes the chain easier to pull." He didn't laugh and I'd rehearsed that gag all week to tell him. That's show business.

"Here," I called as he turned to look at his appointment book. I threw him the rolled *Echo*. He opened it. He couldn't miss the advert I'd placed because I'd ringed it in black. Actually, someone else must have ringed it too because that evening someone else rang about it.

I didn't rehearse that. Honest.

The advert read:

SAMSPADE
GINLEY'S THE NAME
GUMSHOE'S THE GAME
Private Investigations
No Divorce Work
051-246-4379

It was a gag. A birthday present from me, to me. I got the idea from a detective novel. I read a lot of detective novels. American ones all the time, except for Ambler, Greene and Lyall.

So. The psychiatrist was reading the advert and I was on my way home to catch up on a little ironing. I was at home when I got rung.

CHAPTER TWO

I live on the top floor of a house in Gambier Terrace
and my front window faces the Anglican
Cathedral. My room is sort of L-shaped, with one
door leading off to my own bathroom, a hardboard
partition separating it from the kitchen area. The
door leading downstairs to the street faces my bed,
which is below the aforementioned window. In the
corner, by the door, there's a curtained cubbyhole,
which is a wardrobe, and contains my wardrobe. I
hang my trench in there, next to my three-buttoned
suit like the shrink, I'm vintage 1957. Well, I look at
it this way, I'm thirty-one, right? I can't go with
what everyone's wearing these days. Now the late
fifties, that's my time, that's where I'm sticking.
That's where I'm stuck, too, with almost everything, clothes, records – movies I'm stuck with in
the forties. The mountain of trivia that is enclosed

by my skull hails from way back. Anyway, next to my suit is my new tux; I'm still paying for it so it must be new, but I'd give you odds you'd never think so when I've got it on. I've got some good things in my modest little stash, a wall 'phone in the kitchen for instance, and my bookshelves are crammed with several interesting titles – nearly all the Penguin green backs; lots of different books really, a pretty catholic taste that remained when my ugly Catholic religion got the boot. Next to the bookshelves is my record collection and my hi-fi set-up; Thorens 150 deck, Nicco amp, and Celestion 15 speakers for the buffs out there. On the little mantelpiece I have, there is a ten-by-eight of Lauren Bacall, a ten-by-eight of me in my tux – a Jerome's special photograph ("Look showbiz," the photographer said) – a framed colour photograph of the 1970 League Champions, my cufflink collection and a birthday card: "Now you are 31!" A joke one. Ellen sent me that.

I was sitting on the bed ironing (I've got this board that you can adjust to any height – I'm pretty hip to modern methods of cutting the housewife's workload) with the headphones on giving Buddy Holly and the Crickets a play, when I got the ring. Actually a track had finished and I'd taken the headphones off between songs because your ears can sweat something wicked under the old earpieces, when I heard the 'phone. I whipped the 'phones off and crossed to the 'phone, as I will in such instances, and picked it up.

"The Ginley Residence... Just a minute, I'll see if he's in." I crossed to the amplifier and pulled the headphone jack out. "That'll Be the Day" blasted into the room. I went back and picked up the receiver.

"He's in the music room at the moment, running through a number with the band."

I held the receiver towards one of the speakers.

"Can you hear? I'm sorry, you'll have to give me the message, he can't possibly be disturbed." And then this incredibly distant, seemingly sexless voice gave me the message, which I only just got at first go because of the sound of the record. I repeated it. "Exchange Hotel, Room 105, 7.30." The voice said, "Okay?" and rang off. Well, it was my birthday, someone knew I was a pretty lonely fellow, so they were throwing a surprise party. It was no party, but it was a surprise all right.

CHAPTER THREE

The Exchange Hotel backs onto the station of the same name and fronts onto Tithebarn Street. It's big and white and those in the know reckon it to be the best in the city, although I wouldn't know, never having stayed at the joint – only been through it, so to speak. There's an old-fashioned portal and steps leading up to revolving doors, and inside, the reception hall, or foyer, or whatever, is like a green-carpeted, cream-painted, Victorian basketball court without the nets. There's a long desk to the right, and the night I presented myself there was a pretty girl receptionist and an old Welsh one behind it. The latter had a face like a chewed pink caramel, with those blue, rimless, fly-away specs women like her like to sport, and I could tell she was Welsh because she was yacking into the 'phone in that language. The pretty receptionist approached with a smile but Taffy looked up, saw me, and whipping the 'phone down asked me what I wanted sir, gnashing the false choppers. I didn't like her. Some of my best friends are Welsh, and have faces like chewed caramels, and most everyone I know over forty has false choppers and if she's behind a desk earning a wage she's one of us and not THEM, but she came on so obsequious, like it was going out of style. So I gave the pretty one my M.G.M. smile (I'm saving up for caps and a nose job) and asked and was told, prettily, that room 105 was on the first floor, left past the lounge, and that I couldn't miss it. Taffy gave her a look that would have freeze-dried her and I made for the stairs. As I walked up I made a mental note to be nice to Taffy when I came down, being instantly remorseful as I nearly always am when I play hard with anyone. Some people get me like that though; really fix me. It's just that you've got to be on the side of the person who works for a living, the person who hustles a wage. That's a tough enough life. But there are those people for whom service means servility and they seem to love it. Waiters, hotel receptionists, the guys who work the restaurant cars on trains. Not all of them, but why do those who serve *have* to be creeping bastards? Beats me. On the first floor a tray-carrying waiter who was in no way servile marked me down straight away.

"The bandroom's in the basement for tonight," he sneered.

"Why for tonight?"

"We don't run to a proper one so we've put you

in the luggage-room. In the basement. We moved the luggage first, of course."

"Of course."

"We know you bastards. Booze. Groupies."

"Yeah."

He peered at me suspiciously.

"Where's your instrument?"

There was no answer to that, so I flashed my buzzer and he went puce and even showed me past the lounge to the corridor where I could find Room 105. I always carry my buzzer – the clubs I've not been a member of that it's got me into! My friend Arthur showed me how to make a buzzer. It helps if you're unemployed. You see you take your dole card and fold it in half across, and flash the half with the crown on it that says "Official", and people think you are a copper. Arthur had a mate once who used to do it with a ration book (remember them?). But he must have been pretty fast because you have to keep your buzzer in your inside breast pocket for best effect (unless you wear a trench like I do where you can whip it out just below waist level and they've hardly had time to register but still think you're a copper) and one of those old ration books would get stuck if you weren't quick, and by the time you'd got it out you'd have lost your cool. Arthur's mate used to do this to get into clubs, until he got caught. He was very silly really, because he went to this club, whipped out his ration book, got in, and no sooner did he have a bevvy and a bird lined up, than the boss of the place stuck a wad of notes in his hand and gave him the high sign. So it's drinks for all

23

hands and the manager's muttering about how unusual this is and Arthur's mate is throwing money around and dancing with all the birds like he's got first divi on Littlewoods, when the real fuzz arrive and wonder where their kickback is. The manager points out their 'colleague' on the dance floor, with pound notes bulging out of his pockets, buying drinks all round and pulling the birds. The real coppers give him the tap on the shoulder and Arthur's mate, thinking they're muscling in on his talent, tells them to push off or he'll do them for obstruction. They ask which division he's with, and where's his identification, so he smirks and waves his ration book and shouts, "Z Victor One to B.D.!" He got done for impersonating a police officer and asked for two hundred similar offences to be taken into consideration. He got five years. I never forgot that and always stick to dole cards. Anyway you have to cut the ration book into a quarter of its size and stick a photo in it. It's too much trouble.

I knocked on 105 and went in. The room was in pitch darkness, except for a television switched on showing an old movie, and I waited for the lights to come on and everyone to shout "Surprise!" and shower me with presents. Nothing happened, except that from somewhere a voice spoke. A flat, expressionless, business-like man's voice. The voice of a man who, when he told you, you stayed told. The lads had really tried, I thought, they're really making my birthday something to remember.

"Shut the door," the voice said.

I shut it and leant against it.

"Do they charge you extra for the light?" I quipped.

I figured I'd play along until the punch line. Don't spoil a good gag. If your mates have tried, it's only fair you should try too.

"Cut the cracks."

"Just trying to make small talk, mister."

"It's not needed."

"Make your play."

"To the right. There's a dresser," he said. "A package on it. Got it?"

I could make out a chair with a high back now, facing the television, and I could see smoke curling up and smell cigar. I had to give it to the lads, they spared no expense. Or Tommy. This had to be Tommy's doing.

"This the package?" I held it up although he couldn't see it.

"There's no other."

"Okay. What's the pitch?"

"Pitch?" He seemed surprised.

"The job."

"It's all in the package."

"The folding green?"

"What?"

"Money. Twenty dollars a day plus expenses."

I tell you I can pinch material from anywhere. With the best of them.

"Twenty dollars? It's in sterling. That's what was agreed." He seemed really surprised now.

"Don't flip your wig buster," I cautioned him, "I can live with it."

There was a silence for a moment so I looked at

25

the movie on television. Judy Holliday was telling Broderick Crawford that he could use a little education himself if you asked her. One of my favourites. I was just beginning to enjoy it for the fifth time of seeing when the voice cut in sharply. "What are you waiting for?"

"I was just going."

I opened the door. The lights have just got to come on now, I thought.

"Happy Birthday to you, Happy Birthday dear Eddie…" But no.

"I was just going," I said.

"We want results."

I laid it on the line: "Broad at the shoulder and narrow at the hip and everybody knows you don't give no lip, to Big Ed."

No answering laughs, no chuckles, not even a titter. I reached for the light switch; there wasn't one.

"I hope you're as tough as you sound," the voice said.

"Dig this. Nobody steps into this baby's sunshine," I said. Quick as a flash. And stepping into the corridor, I closed the door. I could hear the movie carrying on inside as I waited listening for a few moments. Well, I wasn't going to open the present till I got to the club. I'd let Tommy and his lads see my pleasure as I opened it. I walked down the corridor and as I turned the corner a small neat man wearing a small-brimmed hat passed me.

"Nutters," I laughed and nodded my head towards 105. He looked blankly at me and walked on, but then he didn't know the lads.

26

I had to leg it for the fourteen bus because I was way overdue at the club and having settled into one of those long seats near the exit for a quick jump off for the club, I looked at the package. Brown paper covered, about ten by six, heavily sellotaped. I tore off the tape and lifted a corner of the paper. Inside was a stiff cardboard box. No card. A book. A book for my birthday. They'd never asked me what I read, so, knowing Tommy, it was probably the life of Judy Garland or something. By Mel Torme. Have you read that thing? I'm waiting for the double album to hit the shops. Woolworths of course. On Embassy. Natch. And I like Mel Torme *singing*. The box had a flap, also sellotaped. So I'd sneak a peek and re-wrap and come on at the club as though I'd never looked. Whatever book was inside was stuck, so I turned the parcel upside down and shook it. Out came a photo of a dame and a wad of rubber-banded Bank of Funland notes in tenners, and something else fell out that crashed heavily to the floor, and when I picked it up it was a toy gun. Except when I looked at the notes to see 'pay the bearer ten laughs' I saw the good lady herself's head and ten pounds. And the gun I was holding like Joe Friday was giving the lady opposite a double hernia with fright. And the next thing was that I needed that quick exit from the bus, and I was leaning on a wall miles from the club shaking from fear and anger and wondering what the hell kind of birthday present was this to give a fellow?

CHAPTER FOUR

The club where I work, the Broadway, is set well back from the main drag, which is itself called the Broadway. It's easily missed if you're looking for it, on account of there isn't no sign telling you you've arrived, there's just a gateway at the end of a row of shops which looks like the beginning of a lane. You go up the 'lane', which is in fact a driveway, for fifty yards or so, and you see the magnificence that is the Clubmoor and West Derby Social and Working Man's Club, known as the Broadway. The club has a T shape about it because it is really no more than two brick huts set together – one long, comprising the dressing-rooms, stage and hall, and the other being divided into a bar and small restaurant. I like the place. Tommy Summers, the boss, is regarded by one and all as a fixer, a hustler, and a bad banjo player, but a pretty straight guy.

He part owns the place, so he says, but as nobody ain't ever seen the other part-owner, and Tommy has never so much as vouchsafed the guy's name, everybody reckons the Broadway is all his. He does a pretty fair comedy act of his own (one of those acts that other club acts always put down by saying "it's a good *club* act" – you follow me?) and fronts the band (The Saturated Seven – doesn't that *kill* you?) with his aforementioned banjo playing. You ever seen a band fronted by the banjo player? A bad banjo player? Who doesn't know a crotchet from a hatchet? The band itself is pretty good, given that all hands exhibit a tendency to overblow (to drown the banjo) and includes in its line-up an electric organist who has fathered the best centre-forward in the country, currently playing in the best footballing side in the same.

I got to the club an hour late and really licked. I'd run from where I'd jumped off the bus, not daring to commit myself to any form of transport with the load I was carrying. I opened the door from the car park that led to the passage behind the stage. Off the passage are the three over-sized juke boxes Tommy laughingly calls dressing-rooms and at the end of it is the stairway leading to the stage. Tommy stood there waiting, tuxed and banjoed-up ready to assassinate music, and me for being late. Tommy's only a medium-sized guy with a paunch and a fleshy face with friendly blue eyes, but he can really bawl you out – and bawl me out he did.

"Where the effing, sodding hell have you been, plums?"

"Tommy, I'm in schtuck."

"I'll give you schtuck if you don't get on that sodding stage this minute."

"I'm really in a jam, Tommy."

"The bloody customers are waiting!"

"Just let me use the 'phone and I'll be right with you."

"You'll be right without a job if you don't get up there."

And he was dragging off my coat and pushing me up the stairs. The band were on stage.

"A band number?"

Joe the organist nodded.

I stepped through the curtains. The club was full, and there was a smattering of applause from the person who liked me. I tapped the mike and the sound system whistled.

"Okay, folks, it's time for the band spot now, so if you want to leave it will cost you a pound each, otherwise the doors are barred. Seriously though, folks, they're going to give you a break, because they're going to play in tune. So put your hands over your ears, and without further ado, playing the overture from Brückner's 7th Symphony, I give you our own Saturated Seven! Take it away lads, and bury it!" The audience didn't hear the last bit because on the word "Seven", Jimmy the trumpeter stamped his foot down and the band gave "Way Down Yonder in New Orleans" more than it was worth. As I walked off, Tommy had a second to say "bloody bugger" before he fixed his smile and plucked his note and I had time to realise that I had taken the package on stage. I made for the pay 'phone.

"There's no reply from 105, sir," said the switch-board operator.

"Oh come on, love!"

"I've tried; sir. There's no reply."

"Gimme reception then."

"Reception." It was the Welsh dame.

"I wonder if you could help me –"

"I'll try sir." Milk and honey.

"I picked up something from Room 105 tonight, only I think it was meant for someone else. So what I wondered is, could you give me the name, and I'll send it back?"

"The name sir?"

"The name of the person in 105, lady." Through gritted teeth.

"What name sir?"

I wished I was right behind her now, wrapping the 'phone cord round her neck.

"The name–"

"You see, sir, there's no name to give. *Suite* 105 is vacant, sir."

"Vacant?"

"Yes sir. Vacant. It was vacated this afternoon, sir."

"Did the guy leave a forwarding address? I could post what I got onto him."

"Guy?"

"Don't be thick, love! Did the fellow who had 105 leave a forwarding address?"

"The fellow – ?"

"The man. M-A-N who had the room. R-O-O-M. Room 105. One hundred and–"

"It was a lady, sir."

"It was a fellow! I heard him."

"Sir. Don't try to teach me my job. I have the register in front of me at this moment. A lady, sir. Mrs Blankerscoon. She had the room. She's left."

"Mrs Blankerscoon?"

"Yes, sir."

I put down the receiver and walked to my dressing-room. I sat down in front of the mirror with the three bulbs in it. "Just like the Palladium," Tommy said when he showed me it. He'd stood inside and said "Look at this, Eddie." Then he'd stepped outside and I'd stepped inside to have. a look. That's how big it is. I shook the stuff out of the packet. The gun thumped onto the table in front of the mirror. I took out the photo and the money. I counted the money. One hundred tenners. One thousand not so little, not so lonely pounds. A grand, a gun and a girl. There was a knock on the door. I stuffed the money and the photo back in the package, but the gun wouldn't fit so I stuffed it in my tux pocket. Tommy stood there when I opened the door.

"Do us a favour, Eddie," he said in an ingratiating kind of way.

"Anything. Tommy!"

"Do your effing job!" he shouted. "Get on the effing stage and do your sodding job. Announce the bleeding interval!"

I did. When I got back, Tommy was giving it to Sammy. Sammy's the O.A.P. whose job at the club is to work the handle that opens and closes the curtain. Sammy never has his teeth in and Tommy was threatening him with dismissal.

33

"Where are they?"

"I've lent them to the wife. She's gone to see her sister," Sammy blustered. It's a nightly occurrence. That guy's got more excuses for not wearing his teeth than soft Mick. They're always being mended, or he's lent them out to one of the family, or he put them in the Steradent and put the Steradent in the fridge overnight and they froze solid. Then they burned when he put them in the oven to unfreeze them. I don't believe he's got any at all. He's probably waiting to win the pools and have his gums capped.

I called the bingo after the interval. Tommy presented the lucky winners with bottles of scotch, clocks and giant teddy bears. I announced the acts, stuck a few gags in and the evening was over. I hung around backstage to speak to Tommy and he wanted to speak to me.

"Listen, Tommy."

"No apologies, kid."

"I wasn't going to apologise."

"Charming."

"What I meant was, I was going to apologise, but–"

"Listen, kid, how long have you worked here?"

"Three months."

"Who discovered you in the Labour Club entertaining the O.A.P.s?"

"You did, Tommy."

"Who brought you into the club?"

"You did, Tommy."

"Who gave you the breaks?"

"You did, Tommy."

New readers begin here. The continuing story of Eddie Ginley.

"Can I ask you something, Tommy?"

"Later, kid."

"It's important."

"This is important. I'm going to give you a further break."

"I don't want to go on the door, Tommy."

"You what?"

"I'm five feet seven and timid, Tommy. I'd never make a bouncer."

"I'm going to let you do your act!"

I waited for a catch.

"Yeah?"

"Yes. If you come early tomorrow night. Is that much to ask? Once early in three months?"

"Not really."

"Early tomorrow gets Eddie a spot. Okay?"

"Terrific."

He looked at me quizzically.

"You don't look so happy about it. Isn't it what you want? You're always pestering me about it."

"Next day on your dressing-room they've hung a star." I quipped.

He grinned. "Something like that."

Well, I had to ask him sometime. "Tommy, you gave me the breaks, right?"

"Right!"

"What was I doing but geeing up the O.A.P.s on Thursday nights at the Labour, and maybe addressing envelopes and canvassing every election time, and how often do they come around?"

"Right."

"I was nothing, Tommy, and you made me your announcer and bingo caller. You've been like a father to me, Tommy. I was on the dole. Who subsidised me for the flat? The down payment on my tux? The hi-fi?"

I swear he was nearly crying.

"You're a good kid, Eddie." There was definitely a lump in his throat.

"Tommy. Today is my birthday."

He threw his arms around me and hugged me like a poor man's Zorba the Greek. Then, gripping me by the shoulders with both hands till I winced, he held me at arms' length.

"Kid. What can I say? Happy Birthday!"

"Tommy. The present."

He looked hurt. "It'll come, kid. It'll come. What would you like?"

"Has it come already? Did you give me something already?"

I could see now what I'd have known hours ago had it been Tommy-the-benefactor.

"Like what, Eddie?"

"Like – I dunno. A grand maybe?"

"A grand? A thousand quid? Kid, where would I get a thousand quid from? I haven't opened the fruit machines all week."

"Yeah, Tommy. Goodnight." I went down the passage to the door.

"Hey, Eddie."

I turned. Tommy grinned, "I'll get a present, son. Just don't push. A grand!" He laughed. "Tomorrow night, remember."

"Sure, Tommy. A star is born".

I walked to the bus stop. Bus stop! More money than I'd ever seen before, together, in one place. In my pocket. "I know it's way off the route but do you think the bus could drop me off in Gambier Terrace? 23. There's a tenner in it for you and the driver's trouble. Each." I leaned on the stop. Pay off my tux. Pay off the hi-fi. New set of threads. *Several* new sets of threads. Decorate the pad. Car? No. I can't drive. Sixteen mill prints of "The Maltese Falcon"? "On the Waterfront"? Dubious message in that movie though. "The Blue Dahlia", "The Big Sleep", "The Killing" – what was the copyright position on making prints of movies? Not allowed probably. What was the price if allowed? Prohibitive for sure. Ah well. "Dear Colonel Parker, I am preparing a book to be written by me for a private printing and for sale in a limited, signed (by the author) edition and I wonder if your client would be interested in…

"Chapter One – Genesis"

Ginley: Elvis, may I call you Elvis? Elvis, what does the name Big Boy Cruddup mean to you?

Presley: Why! He's the hidden King of Rock 'n' Roll!

Ginley: They said you was high-classed and that was just *no* lie."

And chicks? I'd be fighting them off my back. You go to the movies? Look out for Susan Anspach. She's in a few American movies these days. Terrific. "You name it Sue baby – it's yours."

You know when you fell for Dale Evans, not Trigger, and you knew you were growing up? I saw this Anspach girl. Just like Ellen she is. Terrific! On a thousand quid? All that? I had to be joking in the first place, and in the second place the money wasn't mine. Who ever'd given it to me had to get it back, because it was a mistake. And yet there I was. Not all that surprised when I come to think of it. After all, hadn't I told the shrink many times that all I needed was a rod, some folding green, a snap-brim fedora, doing my own act in my own club. Shooting my cuffs on the balcony watching Rita Hayworth singing "Put the Blame on Mame" and keeping one eye on the two dealers at the tables. Just like Dick Powell in "Johnny O'Clock". Robert Rossen did the movie. Do you remember Lee J. Cobb as the cop, saying, "I'll give you a break" (so *that's* who Tommy models himself on!) and Dick Powell sneers back, "What? My arms or my legs?" But that was in my *movie* when I was telling the shrink. Not here on a bus. (I was on the fourteen by now). I still didn't feel so funny about having the stuff about my person, as it were – the gun and money and so on. I should have done. I often fantasize on what it's like to be Ball, Harvey or Husband playing a blinder at Wembley, but I'd feel damn funny if I was sitting there in strip. Holding a football.

CHAPTER FIVE

The foyer of the Exchange Hotel was quiet. No one about behind the desk. I walked across the carpet, past the lifts and up the stairs. I walked past the lounge; there was a crowd of businessmen, or reps or whatever monicker they fancy themselves under, braying and knocking back the brandy and giving hell to the night waiter. Ted Heath's Own, at home, in a pack, stripe-suited, club-tied, telling blue jokes and making some poor working sod's life a misery.

The passage down which 105 lay was empty, as I took it swiftly. "SLEUTH SOLVES SLAYING IN CITY STOPOVER – AND GOES BACK TO BINGO. I'm just an ordinary Joe, says 31-today Eddie Ginley."

The door was locked and the handle was one you couldn't turn – the kind you just pull the door locked with. The key does all the work. I listened before trying it and got no sound. The next door along was ajar and since it bore no number I took a chance on it having some relation to 105. It did. I pushed it open, put on the light and found it to be a double bedroom with a connecting door. The connecting door was open. I felt round the jamb for the light and switched it on. There stood the chair the voice had occupied, the huge colour TV he'd been watching, a couch along the wall by the side-board-cum-dresser where the package had been. And nothing else. A smell of cigar smoke, maybe, but not a damn thing else. I looked in the dresser drawers; nothing. Everywhere. On the bedroom dressing table were a few empty cellophane bags such as laundries put on clean shirts. Nothing. Wire hangers in the wardrobe. A big fat 0. I sat on the bed, which was freshly made, and thought, nobody gives anybody such a package then disappears, for nothing.

So for what had I got it? I took the package out again and looked at it. I took out the money and the photo too. The photo was of a young girl, I guessed maybe twenty-one or so. Quite pretty, but nothing to get you up and running to her. I turned the picture over. On the back it said, stamped with crest and all, 'A. Wyatt, Property of Univ. Dept. of Mathematics. Faculty of Science. Not to be removed.' And a number, I suppose a file number. Well, there were two conclusions that followed that discovery one of them was not so very pleasant. Anyway, she got the stuff, if I didn't find out where the person who had the room was and give it all back to them. That got me off the bed and walking.

The night porter was serving more swill to the oiks in the lounge when I passed, and when I got to the foyer there was a guy behind the desk. A small crumpled-looking guy in a light blue suit, with a shock of grey hair in a quiff and big black specs. An ancient teddy boy perhaps, so maybe, a friend. He looked up.

"You still here? I thought the band had gone." That tux.

"I'm enquiring after a friend, actually."

"A resident in the hotel?"

"Checked out today."

"Expecting a message? There's nothing in the pigeon holes." He gestured behind him to the key rack and pigeon holes for letters. "Nothing on the notice board either. I always look. I'm the telephonist really, I just stand here for Bob, he's the night porter in the lounge. I see all the visitors out, and let the night-birds in. I lock up about three. Well, it helps him out see?"

The story of his life.

"I'm really hoping to discover if she left a forwarding address."

"Like I said, you can see there's no messages."

I pulled a face. He smiled knowingly.

"Girlfriend is she? Let you down?"

"Oh. No. It's business."

"What was the room number?"

"105."

He leafed through the ledger in front of him.

"Blankerscoon?"

41

"That's the one."

He whistled through his teeth. "Look at that!" He stabbed angrily at the page. "It shouldn't be allowed, that." I grabbed the book and turned it round. There was the name all right. Blankerscoon. And where it said home address, there was nothing. This wasn't Ginley's night. The little fellow was beside himself with anger. "These girls are told. *Told* always to make sure these details are filled in."

"Shouldn't the guest do it? I mean if they leave it out when they check in, the receptionist would surely notice."

"Oh, no. You see, guests don't write in here. Look." He produced a card. "They fill one of these in, address, nationality and room number, and the girl copies it up later. You see if a lot of people check in at once there'd be a queue here, so you give them one of these cards to fill in at their leisure and drop back at the desk."

That didn't help me. He thought for a moment.

"That Welsh get. I bet it was that Welsh get."

"Sure."

"Was it important?"

"Only vital, dad, only vital." It was going to be a long night for both of us, so I thought I'd give him something to talk about. I flashed my buzzer. He nodded and smiled.

"I can't say anything more."

"I understand, son."

"Thanks anyway, pop. Goodnight."

"Goodnight."

I walked to the revolving doors.

42

"You know something?" he said. I turned.

"What dad?"

"You've made my night."

"Really?"

"Really," he smiled. "It's years since I've seen the old dole card trick."

So. You win a few, you lose a few. That's my motto.

The grand piano I sat at was nice, and so it should be since it must have cost twice as much as what I had in my pocket. It was a grand worth two, you might say. The rest of the room was just expensive – two overstuffed chesterfields, two small, steel-and-glass occasional tables – and a steel-and-leather chair that looked as though you'd perform a minor operation on yourself if you sat in it. I didn't. Leather-bound volumes filled the shelves – all bought by the yard like the furniture. The piano music I was playing was nice too, even though I say it myself, a selection of oldies-but-goodies like "Where or When", "The Way You Look Tonight", "Polka Dots and Moonbeams" – no rubbish. Then the door opened, someone came in and crossed the room and switched off the gram, so I stopped miming and swivelled round the piano stool. She took off her headscarf and shook her ash-blonde hair free, then took a packet of fags from her pocket; stuck one between her full red lips and lit it with the half-ton of silver on the gram that masqueraded as a lighter. She looked really cool, but why shouldn't she? I'd only broken into the house on a friendly basis.

43

"Who are you?" I asked.

"I live here," she said.

"He plays good piano, Bud Powell, doesn't he?" I said.

"Who's he?" she asked.

"You just switched him off," I said.

"Want to hear anything special?"

"Play 'Melancholy Baby'," she said.

"How does it go?" I asked.

"How the hell did you get in?" Losing interest in the tune.

"Rain or hail or sleet or snow, the Pinkertons are on the go – I broke in the back way with a little piece of plastic I carry round for such purposes. What do they call you?"

"Guess," she said.

"Blonde, blue-eyed, small, lightweight and slim. They must call you Slim."

"I've been called worse especially by you," she said.

"Hello, sister-in-law," I said.

"Hello, Eddie."

"Hello, Ellen," I said.

We often talk like that in our family, at least Ellen and I used to talk like that. Till she married my brother William. He's the only other member of our family. He never talks like that.

She stubbed out the cigarette, untied the belt on the expensive suede coat she was wearing and threw it carelessly so that it missed anything it was aimed at, like one of the chesterfields, and fell on the floor. People with money can do things like that.

44

"People with money can do things like that," I said.

"Like what?" she asked.

"Not hanging their coats up. Where's William?"

"Out."

"You married the wrong brother, kid. I wouldn't leave you alone to be threatened in this manner."

There was an embarrassed silence because we both knew what she was going to say next.

"I didn't get a better offer," she said, and walked out of the room. I followed her downstairs to where they kept the kitchen. She was filling the kettle at the tap. I leant in the doorway and pulled out the gun as she plugged the kettle in.

"Those were frontier towns, ol' pardner,
'Twas a game of take and give;
An' the one who could draw the fastest,
Was the only one who'd live."

"Did you make that up?" she said.

"No. I stole it from a book. I just thought of it when I got my gun out."

She grinned, "You haven't changed."

"I'm a year older."

"You get my card?"

"Yeah."

"Happy Birthday."

"Thanks, kid."

"We haven't got you anything yet."

"*We*?"

"*We* haven't got you a present."

"I'm surprised *we'd* discussed it."

"William's really fond of you deep down, Eddie."

"He'd be fonder of me if I was six feet down and covered with soil."

If someone makes a remark like that to you about your nearest and dearest there's precious little you can say. She said nothing so we sat down and had tea.

It had always been understood by one and all that Ellen and I would marry. We'd been going together since we were kids. We'd always knocked around together. Brother William had knocked around with us too, even though three years older, a sort of threesome, except that it had always been Ellen and me who were the couple and William the gooseberry. He's still a gooseberry in my book, but he got to marry my girl. How he got to marry is difficult to explain. Even when I was still studying for 'A' levels and University, spending a lot of time in the Picton library, and William seemed to have a lot of free time from the shipping office where he worked, it was still Ellen and me, though he naturally took her around a bit. I wouldn't say I wasn't the marrying kind, I'm pretty normal, I think, and regard marriage and kids as the pretty normal ambition of most pretty normal blokes. But it got to be that we'd been knocking around for going on fifteen years, even living together for a good part of that when I was away at college, and she began to get a bit anxious about the lack of a ring. It bothered me less and less as the time went on because I, unconsciously I suppose, more or less considered what we had was as legal as it needed to be. Unless

46

kids came along, and they didn't. The crunch came when we went to see a movie and a girl in it made a remark about when was the wedding going to be because they'd been going together for years and she didn't want the rice to knock her down. Ellen took this as her cue – we had a row, and that was it. I must have inflicted a pretty deep wound on her because next thing I know, her and William are up and marrying and I realise I'm not only losing my girl, but losing her to my brother, who suddenly appears to be a man of some considerable substance. Owning his own business. Exporting and importing. Botha Ltd.

Not that relations with *him* had been anything other than strained when Ellen wasn't around. What can you say about a brother who doesn't turn up for his parents' funerals? Except that he's the perfect argument for family planning. After all, my father had had the courtesy to die within a year of my mother and it had been a racing certainty that he was going to go soon anyway, so you'd think William would have kept his appointments down. Just in case. If only to visit the old man in hospital, which he didn't do either. Try explaining night after night for seven months to a dying man why his eldest son can't make it in to see him. And those nights he's delirious with drugs to kill the pain, try acting the part of your brother come to see his old man. Then after the old guy's dead and buried, try keeping your love for your brother going, and let him marry your girl (Ellen always cared for Dad, she came to the hospital with William's lame excuses, she knows what a

47

schnook she's married) and see if you don't end up under a psych having kept your neurosis down to hypochondriasis. It's not easy. Anyway, forget it. It doesn't bother me so much any more. Except when I look at her.

"Did you come to see William?" she said on the rim of her cup.

"Him? If he were dying the priest wouldn't come to see him." That hurt her. As usual. So I said I was sorry.

"Sorry."

"That's okay." It wasn't.

"How's the club?"

She knew everything.

"You know everything."

"I hear rumours," she said.

"The psychiatrist?"

"That too," she admitted. "What's he like?"

"Oh. Off his head."

She laughed.

"I wish I had you in the audience when I do the gags."

"Don't they laugh at you?"

"Yeah, at me, not at the jokes."

She laughed again. I looked at her.

"Gee, kid, you're lovely when you're mad."

She frowned, "Mad at what?"

She was supposed to laugh at that, too. Never mind.

"What's that for?" she pointed. I'd been drinking the tea with one hand and holding the gun with the other.

"Shtick 'em up," I lisped. She laughed then.

"Listen. It's a real one, you know."

"Even you're too old for a toy one, Eddie. Put it away."

"Same old Ellen."

"I don't get you."

" 'Put it away.' Same old Ellen. Get it?"

"No."

"Then forget it."

We fell quiet a bit while I mused on things. Like how did she see me? How did any of my friends see me? I know I had, and have, a reputation for jokes – okay, for poor jokes – but shouldn't it have fazed her that I had admitted to having psychiatric treatment and was waving a gun about? A real gun. I saw it was a real gun from the kick off. Couldn't she see it?

"It's got bullets in."

"What has?" Oh come on!

"The *gun*. This thing."

"So?" A pause. Then, "Why didn't you come to the wedding?"

I am opposed to the women's liberation movement not because I do not believe women should not be liberated but because I believe all mankind should be liberated. One day the hammer and anvil of capitalism and Stalinism will be done away with. That's socialism. I have an education, you know. The point that I am trying to make is that all those jokes about women's logic – women drivers, mothers-in-law et al, make me sick. They're not important in themselves but only as a manifestation of a deep-seated misogynism that many men have. But, given all that, perhaps those red-nosed

49

comics had a point when they joked about the way women think, because I can't think of many *guys* I know at whom you could point a gun, if only in fun, tell them it was real and had bullets in it, who would change the subject *completely*.

"I was waiting for the second house," I said lamely.

"Second house at a wedding?"

"I sent a telegram."

"To William. I quote : 'The best man lost. Congratulations schmok. Eddie.' Was that nice?"

"I told the guy at the Post Office that 'schmok' was Latin for love. They're very hot on obscene messages sneaking through."

"What *is* a schmok?"

"The guy you married."

"He didn't like it."

"He's got no sense of humour."

She looked at me, "You think I have?"

I said, "Why else would you marry him?"

"Well! Well! Well!" said somebody else, so I looked up from pouring a second cup of tea and there stood my brother. Beautifully suited. The same handsome Ginley features as myself, I lied easily, and though looking perpetually worried and going grey because of it, he still managed an overall air of smug well-being. He walked to the sink and got himself a glass of water to drink with the tablet he took from a small gold dispenser in his waistcoat pocket. I didn't stick around for long after he came in, so I'll just have to give you the dialogue for a whiff of filial affection. I'm speaking first.

"The Brother Grimm. Feeling better?" I asked, as he swallowed his pill.

"Only when I see the back of you."

"Welcome to Rancho Notorious, William."

"A family reunion is it?"

"Quick as a flash." I snapped my fingers.

"What do you want?"

"What do brothers want brothers for, Billy Boy? Chew the fat, have a drink. Swap old jokes."

"Did you invite him?" he said to Ellen.

"He was here when I arrived."

"In my house?"

"Playing your piano, William." Near enough anyway.

"I suppose you want money."

"When did I ever come to you for money?"

"The night before my wedding." Everything 'my', never 'our'.

"I needed that."

"To send me abusive telegrams?"

"I used my own money for the telegram, I used yours to go away."

"You were supposed to be my best man."

"I don't like sad occasions."

"You! You don't like anything that means putting yourself out, being responsible, working."

"You can talk, Billy baby. Anyway, I'm working now."

"A working man's club?"

"It's not Las Vegas."

"It never will be."

"Goodnight, Ellen."

I got up and made it to the door. He stopped me.

51

"Wait. We don't see you for a year. You must want something."

I turned to look at him, "I got given something tonight and I'm just checking to see if anybody I know gave it to me."

"A present was it?" he sneered.

"You could call it that."

"The day I give you a present, pigs will fly." That's his idea of snappy repartee.

"Thanks for the flying pig." Us Ginleys should stay out of the repartee business. I walked out.

CHAPTER SIX

Have you ever had to look for anyone? I mean someone you don't know and have never met before. Of course, if you have a photograph of the person you're looking for and the name it must be much easier. If you've got the photograph, the name, the place where the person studies, it must be a doddle. It must be for anyone of normal intelligence.

You're looking for a student in a university, so where do you go? The Students' Union, natch. The secretary, you ask? You've got it. Easy. Suppose the secretary can't spare the time. Suppose you don't want to ask the secretary in the first place because, after all, the points you want to bring up with the student you're looking for are a gun and a thousand pounds, and maybe the student you're looking for has a perfectly innocent explanation for it all and it's her property, and she wouldn't like it nosed around that she owns it, either.

A mere matter of six hours later, including a break for lunch, I found my quarry. I'd just hung around the foyer of the union showing the photograph of the girl and asking, getting a lot of funny looks because I must have looked like a raw recruit to the Special Branch, and eventually finding the chick. What did it say on the back of the picture? 'A. Wyatt. Property of Univ. Department of Mathematics. Faculty of Science.' And where did I eventually find her? In the library of the Department of Mathematics, working. All that I can say in my defence is that there are maybe ten thousand students at the University, give or take a few. A lot of them use the union and I must have asked a good proportion of them. You could do better? You try sleuthing for a living. I'm only an amateur.

It wasn't such a big library, more like a reading room in fact, but if had all the usual attributes – lots of books and quiet. Except for the bloke who's got a cold, and his friend, Mr Echo. I remember when I was studying in that monument to learning in East Yorkshire, that if you were trying to work in the library there were always two coughers. One in front of you and one behind, and they always coughed within seconds of each other. Just like the Maths library when I entered. The student who had been kind enough to escort me to the building pointed out the top of a head which was bobbing about behind a table about twenty yards away from me. I walked towards it and sat in the place immediately opposite to it. I looked around. Lots of students earning those pittances called grants that the Neanderthal Right thinks they ought to be made to pay back. For all those sit-ins and demonstrations and for being layabouts. Don't they know how hard it is to organise demonstrations, even amongst students? Don't they know it's usually the brightest and hardest working students who go on demonstrations? I pushed aside the bookrest and saw a lot of hair. The hair went on working for a bit then looked up, saw the book was gone and I was staring at her. She was about twenty-one as I'd surmised from the photograph – which didn't do her justice because she was very pretty. She wore her hair long, had a good hooter and strong teeth and over her deep black eyes and perched on that aforementioned hooter she wore what you call granny specs.

What followed – the short sharp exchange – was one of those experiences I'd longed for all my life. You know how you lie in bed plotting how you'll speak to a girl the following day – you'll say this and she'll say that and so on? And how it never works out because you feel foolish, or she doesn't react in the way you expected or because the opportunity to speak to her never arises? This day was different, and the good thing was that I didn't fancy her, not knowing her before, and hadn't rehearsed anything to say.

She reached for the book but I kept my hand on the rest.

"Ginley," I said, really tough. I was tired and cheesed off through looking for her, so I probably *sounded* tough. Does that make sense?

"Ginley what?" she said. Dead cool.

55

"Ginley. Colon. Eddie."

"Wyatt. Colon. Alison. Go away." She moved the bookrest back and continued writing her essay or notes or whatever. I pushed the bookrest to one side again and she looked up angrily.

"Take off your specs," I said.

She looked at me for a long moment; then slowly, very slowly, took off her glasses.

"Is it Rag Week, already?"

I pushed the photograph across to her.

"I wouldn't know, lady. Is this your mug shot?"

She looked at it. "Where did you get?"

"I'm asking the questions," I said, pulling back the photo.

She put down her pen. "Yes, it's my picture. If I autograph it, will you go away?"

"I'd rather talk."

She looked at me, "What if I framed it?"

"Where would you hang it?" I can push the sarcasm about, too.

"Anywhere you want, Mr Ginley, so push off."

I didn't. She put her glasses on again, folded her arms and leant on the table.

"Okay, what's the beef, Ginley?"

"What's the game, Miss Wyatt?"

"What game?" Patiently as if asking a child.

I leant across the desk. "The game. The gun."

"What gun?"

"The gun, the money and this photo, what are they for?"

"What are you talking about?"

"Three strikes, you're out, Miss Wyatt."

"I'm sorry. I'm not very good at quizzes."

56

There was a loud complaint from behind me. "For Christ's sake, this isn't the debating society!"

I turned to see an African student glaring at me from a seat by the door. I gave him a sweet smile and turned again to the girl. She was sitting back now, arms folded still, as though waiting for the start of the main feature, so I had to lean right across the table and raise my voice to a louder whisper.

"Don't act dumb with me, lady. Someone gave me your photo, a gun and a thousand pounds at the Exchange Hotel. They rang my number and asked for Ginley the private eye – that's me, see, or rather it is and it isn't, because I'm not really a private eye. Do you follow so far?"

"I'm *listening*, Mr Ginley. Do I have to follow?"

I tried a snarl. "Yes, you do, lady, because the point is that this is either a huge joke and I'm slow to get the punch line, or I'm being suckered into something. Either way it involves you. So, what is it? Do I have to give you the stuff or is the grand payment for knocking you off with the gun?"

She looked up at the ceiling in a bored fashion then looked at me again.

"You finished?" she asked, very politely.

"No. I want a few answers and I suggest we step outside so that you can give them."

"I've got work to do," she said.

"And I've got this," I replied and produced the gun. She didn't bat an eyelid.

"You had better put it away," she said, "people might notice."

I grinned at her. "I'll tell them I'm studying criminology."

It didn't get the yock from her I expected. Not even a small yock, not the slightest titter. She just leaned across the table, apparently about to yawn and making no attempt to conceal it.

"Mr Ginley," she said, "Whilst your conversation has a certain flavour that is very much to my taste, nevertheless, mundane as it sounds, I have an essay to write and I cannot spare the time to talk with you." And so saying she pulled back the bookrest, picked up her pen and resumed work. I sat there looking stupid. I'd made my play, displayed my gat and got a fat nothing in response. I could, of course, walk round the table, jam the gun against her spine and tell her to get moving, I thought, but somehow I don't think she'd go. Besides which it had taken a lot to pull the gun out and I had used up all my toughness. All I wanted was to get the hell out and go home. The bookrest moved. She peered at me.

"Where can we meet?"

"My place."

"Where's that?"

"23, Gambier Terrace. Top flat."

"When?"

"After eleven tonight."

She smiled. "You wouldn't be trying to proposition me, would you, Mr Ginley?"

"You ever heard the expression 'fat chance', lady?" I can give with the best of them when it's called for.

"You'll be there then, will you?"

"If I'm not, just walk in, I'll leave it unlocked."

"I'll be there," she said.

I stood up and leaned across the table.

"No foul-ups, Miss Wyatt," I said, all tough again, but she ignored me and started to write again.

I turned and walked to the door. As I passed the end table the African student hissed at me, "You're no student!"

I shoved my mug into his and said, I thought, very coolly, "No, I'm the great white hope." Then I walked out. I'm aces with crushing remarks.

The Morris Minor pulled off the street onto the billis, a great expanse of waste land waiting for the speculators or the University to move in and stick up concrete blocks. That's progress. I'm not against it but they've torn the heart out of this city and stuck it on the East Lancs road. People used to live here. The streets still survive but the houses don't. The houses that were here before were mostly jerry-built and fit only for the rats that infested them even while people still lived in them. Sure a few houses still survive, mostly in the old squares – Faulkner, Abercromby – but now they are University departments or seedy hotels, or consulates. Myrtle Street, Vine Street, most of Bedford Street gone. Chadwick Street gone, just leaving a hole. Where I stood now, in the middle of what had once been all those streets, was a single bare tree, ridiculously erect amongst nothing. Nature's last stronghold – ah! Symbolism's a lot of crap. Out in Kirkby, Croxteth, Southdene and Cantrill Farm, Dead Man's Gulch, live the people of the city, in great concrete battleships, with nothing to do but watch the television and let their kids kick hell out of the telephone boxes and bus shelters. They're not grateful you see. I'm saying nothing that's new, except that one day we won't stop at knocking down the old houses, we'll knock down the system. That's not new, either, but it's a good idea.

Arthur Cubbin got out of the Morris and walked over to where I stood against the tree. He hasn't changed much in all the years we've known each other, hasn't Arthur. He still wears, as he did that day, his hair in a D.A., still has the Buddy Holly spectacles, still wears a slim-jim, drainpipes and big suede shoes. He stopped a few years earlier than me in the clothes sense, did Arthur. Although he's respectable now, years ago he was the nearest thing to a criminal I knew. He used to work the 'chuckling box' racket, as he put it. He had a little minivan and he'd drive around new estates knocking on doors. If a woman answered, he'd check she was on her own, then tell her he'd come to fix the television. Of course, the woman would say that she hadn't 'phoned for a repair man, and he'd tell her then that it was all part of the service – the company were doing a spot check. He'd whip in the house, switch the 'brilliance' knob down or the sound off when the woman wasn't looking and, as he put it, he'd be away. When they wanted to know what was wrong, he'd say that the 'chuckling box' had gone, and if they asked what that meant, he'd have a few phoney technical terms ready, like 'the upper left-flange cross sprocket' or something. He'd tell them he didn't have the stuff in his van to fix the set, but he would take it back to the shop and do it. He'd promise, cross his heart, to have it back by tea-time. The woman would make Arthur swear that he wouldn't forget and off he'd go with the set. It didn't always work, of course, but in a good week he could 'take' about twelve or fifteen sets. Never caught, was Arthur. God knows how he missed it, though, because he had some near escapes in that racket. He had to be made to stop, though – you imagine coming home from a day slogging your guts out, looking forward to *Match of the Day* or something, and finding your telly gone. Try explaining that to the branch manager of the Granada. Arthur works for the council now.

"Hello, Eddie," he said with that sly grin he used on the housewives.

"Hello, Arthur."

"Haven't seen you since the World Cup and up you pop on the telephone."

We shook hands the way old mates do.

"What about the shot Pele hit from behind the half-way line, eh? Made that goalie drop his ollies."

"Yeah. Here." I shoved the gun at him.

He looked at it, opened the chamber, shut it and gave it back.

"Well?" I asked.

"It's a Smith and Wesson, five shot, walnut stocked, police special. Or if you want to be *really* technical, it's a Detective Special. American job. You can see for yourself – look at the address on the barrel."

He walked around the tree and back again.

"Nice day," he said.

61

"Anything else?"

"Yeah," he said, "they're hard to get hold of and they make bloody big holes in things, and people. If it had bullets, of course."

"It did. I took them out. How much?"

He looked at me questioningly. "Selling it? In this town? Nothing. You might find a nutter to take it, but none of the serious lads would touch it."

"It's not a gun town, is it, Arthur?"

"It's not really a gun *country* yet, Eddie. Thank God. Of course you'd probably get a price for it in London. Thirty or forty quid, maybe sixty or seventy because it's new, but I don't know, Eddie, I only worked the telly racket, I was never villainous. Why do you have to ask me?"

I shrugged, "I don't exactly know, mate."

"You're not really selling it, are you?" he said.

"It's not mine to sell. I was given it. I'm trying to find out why. I thought you might have heard if a Smith & Wesson or whatever it is had come into town."

He stared at me. "Bloody Hell, Eddie, who do you think I am? Legs Diamond? 'Psst! There's a .38 come into town, tell Arthur.' Gee whiz! I'm an ex-telly thief working for the council. I wouldn't *know* which way is up if I wasn't told. I wouldn't know about guns, Eddie. I don't *want* to know, so if you've got one, I haven't seen you. Ta-ra la!"

And with that he walked to his car. I followed him. He stopped at the car door.

"Take care, Eddie. Give us a ring. Come and see the wife and kids. Don't bring the hardware. Get rid of it."

"Sure, Arthur."

He stood there, I stood there.

"Going back to work?"

He gestured around him, "I'm at work. See all those condemned houses? They're my responsibility. I go around seeing they're not broken into. You were very lucky to catch me in the office."

"Cushy, is it?" I said for something to say.

"Eighteen hundred a year," he said.

"What are they doing with the condemned houses, Arthur?"

"They're knocking them down and building slums," he said.

"All these are yours, eh?"

"Yeah," he said.

"Don't lose them," I said.

"See you, then!" he said.

"Not if I see you first."

He grinned, got into his car and drove away.

I stopped at the dock gate. The policeman came out of his hut and I pointed to the warehouse about a hundred yards ahead, at the black-coated figure standing there.

"See that ugly fellow over there? He asked to see me." The policeman looked and William raised his arm to signal that it was okay to let me on the docks. I went through the gate and walked over to big brother. He stood on the ramp that ran right round the big warehouse, hands in pockets, looking mean. I reached him and he looked down at me.

"Well," he said, not as a question, more as an expression of his continuing surprise that I exist.

"Well," I said.

"You always have that look on your face as though you want something but you're not letting on what it is."

I looked up at him.

"I want to know what you want. That's what I want now. And why you couldn't tell me over the 'phone."

He didn't answer but reached down his hand to help me up the ramp.

"A helping hand from my brother? Whatever next?" I sneered. I love sneering now and again, especially at William.

"Come on," he said, and set off walking round the corner of the warehouse on to the docks proper. "Ships," he nodded, at the ships in dock.

"Go on," I said, "you're having me on."

He looked at me for a minute. "Hang on," he said, and walked over to a man who had come out of the warehouse. He gave the man something and I caught him saying, "Go on – put it away." I swear the man touched his forelock before he turned and went back into the warehouse. Well, the fight is on against the backward element in the working class as much as the bourgeoisie, I thought. "Come on," William said again, and we walked down the dock.

"I'm not paying a social visit, William."

"It was your birthday yesterday," he said.

"I never noticed."

"I suppose I ought to wish you Happy Birthday."

"Don't crack your jaw getting it out."

He stopped, stuck his hand in his pocket and came out with an envelope which he gave to me. I took it.

"Happy Birthday," he said.

I looked at the envelope, a thin, flat envelope.

"Couldn't you find anything smaller?" I asked.

"I'm trying to be nice." And as if to prove it, he attempted a smile. It didn't come off.

"I knew you were trying something." I was trying to be nasty. It came off. "That fellow back there. You gave him something. Was it his birthday, too?"

William stopped. "That was business. This." He stuck out a foot and kicked a box that held up a pile of similar boxes. The boxes were about three by two by two. They were marked 'Gardening Tools', and stamped underneath 'BEIRA'.

"What's Beira?" I asked him.

"Not 'what', 'where'. It's a port in Mozambique."

"They do a lot of gardening in Mozambique?" I asked.

He smiled. "A lot of gardening."

"What's wrong? You're smiling."

He stopped smiling.

"I knew it couldn't last," I said and we looked at each other like two boxers sparring for an opening.

"Okay, I'll tell you," he said. "I want that ad out of the paper." I held up the envelope.

"This the price?"

"No."

"No dice."

"I want the ad out of the paper."

65

"You're not hearing so well. I said no dice."

"I want it out. I don't like people ringing me up and asking for the private investigator."

"Then they should look at the paper more closely. It's my telephone number in the ad. They should ring me up. I'm losing work."

"Work? They're not offering work, they're jokers, they think it's funny. They're making mock of my name. I won't have it. The name Ginley means something in this city. I don't like it being ridiculed."

"No kidding? Then tell your mates to stop ridiculing it. They must know you if they ring you up over my advert. And as for *your* name, Billy baby, it's my name too. I don't like it being ridiculed either. The fact that you have the name too ridicules it in my eyes. And another thing."

"Yes," he said.

"I don't like people ringing me up with crooked deals." That shook him.

"Crooked deals?"

"Gardening tools for Mozambique." There went my sneer again.

"You're in trouble," he said.

"You asking me or telling me?"

He looked at me for a long moment and then said, carefully, "I could offer you a job."

"Where? You bought a mortuary?"

"I'm trying to help you, Eddie. I think you need it."

"Save it, William. I take the ad out of the paper and you give me a job. Get someone to give you what you want and you give them a break. You

66

were a schnook when you were a kid and you're a schnook now you've grown up."

"You've really had a go at me, haven't you?"

"You deserve it." I stuffed the envelope into his overcoat pocket.

"You don't want my present?"

"Save it. It's the thought that counts." And I turned and walked off the dock. Brothers, brothers, there were never such devoted brothers.

CHAPTER SEVEN

For my debut at the Broadway as a fully-fledged comic, as promised by Tommy, I was an hour early. He nearly fell over. I don't know what it is about me and work that makes me late; perhaps it's a deep-seated, yet unconscious, aversion to it. I must ask the psych sometime or have I asked him already and forgotten the answer? The forgetting would be part of the aversion too. William would call it a perversion, maybe. I know I lack that bourgeois sense of duty that makes people battle on working when they've got the 'flu or something.

At the Broadway I get terribly nervous before I go on, even if all I have to say is "Ladies and Gentlemen, I give you the Saturated Seven", or just call the bingo. I was nervous that night all right, for my first act. I went to the lav about nine or ten times, chain smoked, had a couple of quick snifters that Sammy-the-curtain-raiser got for me. Then my big moment, on stage behind the closed curtains as Tommy announced me, checking my fly, clearing my throat – I always get catarrh when I'm due on stage. Nervousness again. Normally, I can hardly be heard through the first joke in my act because I think I'm going to be sick with it (catarrh, not the joke), but if that first one gets a yock then I'm all right. If it doesn't, it's murder. I do okay though, usually.

Tommy blew into the mike to establish that it worked and said:

"Now folks, I want you to sit back, relax and give a warm welcome to a lad making his debut here tonight. You've seen him before, of course, but now he's here to amuse. A big hand for a kid with a big future – our own Eddie Ginley!"

Just time to run my tongue around my mouth, try a hawk or two to bring up the catarrh and I was on and Tommy was gripping my arm and whispering:

"Three minutes, Eddie, more in the second half and don't forget to announce the stripper!"

Then loudly, clapping as he backed off stage, "Eddie Ginley, Ladies and Gentlemen!"

Well, there was a minute gone of my act already. Did I have enough gags for the rest? Anyway, when the applause, which had been more than polite but less than a standing ovation, died down, I pointed to stage left where Tommy had exited and said:

"Tommy Summers, folks! You may not remember the face, but you never forget the suit." That got a small yock and I was away. The rest of my act? I'll give you a representative sample of gags, but don't bother to take your teeth out, because you won't swallow them laughing.

Gags 1, 2, 3 and 4 (I'm telling you this in case you don't think there are any – or can't distinguish one from the next) :

"Seriously, folks, Tommy's a great guy and he can't be blamed for not buying a new suit. He's not mean, he's just got short arms and deep pockets. He went to the doctor once with a terrible pain. 'Is it my heart, doctor?' he asked. 'No,' said the doctor, 'you've just got angina of the wallet.' It's not funny is it? And he's been in trouble with the police – he got caught breaking into a pound note... got off with a caution though, because it was his first offence."

Gag 5 : "We were in Burma during the war. My dad owned a bamboo mine. When the war started the Army didn't know who it was fighting, the Chinese or the Japanese. So to find out who was the enemy they used to take their socks off, roll them up into a ball and throw them over the trenches. If they started juggling with them, they were Japanese, if they came back washed and ironed, they were Chinese."

I did another gag about squeezing a canary into a drink and it was time to announce the stripper.

"Ladies and Gentlemen, the following act has done more for dancing than Fred Astaire and Ginger Rogers put together, and they were never put together like her. She fainted in here last week and it took four men to carry her out. Two abreast.

71

The Queen of the Strip, Miss Mellodie Damoore!"

I was off. I'd done my first solo spot as a comic. The audience? Laugh? I thought they'd never start… I'd done okay, considering the jokes dated from some time prior to the Norman Conquest. They probably did and all. I saw a programme on television once, about a Viking settlement they'd found on an island off the coast of Scotland. A whole settlement it was, and on the walls was a whole lot of Viking writing, so they rushed up the scholars to translate. All it said on the walls was "Olaf was here", and "I shout and scream and jump for joy because I was here before Olaf." What had been discovered was a Viking bog, and the second thing they'd discovered was that the Vikings couldn't rhyme. Straight up.

I came off stage looking for Tommy and congratulations. He was just putting down the pay 'phone and he was looking as though he'd been told he had to pay his artistes.

"How did I go, Tommy?"

He just stood there staring at the 'phone as though I wasn't around. I put a hand on his shoulder and he jumped like I'd startled him.

"How did I go?"

"Great, kid. Great." He spoke without conviction.

"Was I that bad?"

"No, no, it was great. Come into my office."

"Sure, I'll just get a fag."

"Okay." Then off he went.

I got a cigarette from the dressing-room and made to follow him. At the door that led from backstage into the club, old Sammy grabbed my arm.

"Fantastic, Eddie. Fantastic. I've not seen an act like you've just done since Arnold Quickfeather."

"Arnold Quickfeather?" He was a new one on me.

"You've heard of Arnold Quickfeather. 'Fun with a Bun.' He used to leap out in front of this huge prop bun on stage."

"Oh! *That* Arnold Quickfeather."

"I knew you'd remember him," Sammy said, "he was a comedian, too."

"He'd have to be."

"Terrific, he was." Sammy wiped away a tear. "Laugh? you'd never credit it. Now I'm going to 'phone up this friend of mine who writes a column. 'Round the Clubs', he calls it. You must get a mention in the *press*!"

A mention in the press! I could see it all :

LINES FROM LANCS
Miss Mellodie Damoore, just back from a roaringly successful tour of Japanese working men's clubs displayed her pulchritudinous charms for all to see at the Broadway Club last week. Solid support was rendered by a variety of acts all hosted by genial Tommy Summers. Way down the bill, but up-and-coming, was 31-year-old bingo calling funster Eddie Ginley...

As I walked through the club and the bar beyond it, quite a few people said "Great" and "Well done, Eddie", which, even if they were lying, engendered in me a small feeling of euphoria. I reached

Tommy's office door. I knocked. He called me and in I went. He sat behind his desk counting the take – fivers, oncers, ten bob pieces and shillings everywhere. He waved me to his private bar and I poured myself a lemonade. I don't drink really. I started not drinking when I got pills from the shrink, because you can't go out on the bevvy when you are stoked up on librium and valium. It's dangerous. So I gave up booze and now I seem to have given up both. One day I'll give up ciggies and I'll be laughing.

"Have a seat, kid, I'll be with you in a minute," said Tommy, as he counted the money.

"Take your time, Tommy," and I browsed around his office – which is nothing to browse around. Apart from his desk, there's his safe and his bar – one of those small, padded, dimpled bars you see in footballers' semis, and that's all. Except that all four walls are covered with photographs. Photographs of Tommy. And all the stars. Together. I looked at one, "To the kid from Scotland Road from the kid from Hoboken. Love, Frank" it was signed, and there was Tommy in the picture with his arm around Sinatra. "To Tommy. Lo chayim, Danny", and there was Danny Kaye enjoying a joke! I looked up from one of those photos – "You've scored a few goals in your time, Tommy. Regards, Pelly."

"None of the footballers can spell can they, Tom?"

"That's a disgrace, that one. I told the fellow, 'What am I paying you for, wack, if you're going to cock up the spelling?' I got it for nothing."

"Doesn't anyone notice that all the stars write with the same biro, and you're wearing the same suit in every picture?"

"An old man's fantasy, Eddie." He smiled.

"Tommy, you're only forty-two."

"In the club game, multiply that by three."

I sat down. He finished counting and looked up.

"I'd be lost without the fruit machines here."

"Would you?"

"Yeah. The stripper's great, isn't she?"

"You've seen one breast, you've seen both of them." I paused. "Tommy, what is it?"

"What's what?"

I put my drink on the table.

"You've counted the same pile of money three times, so what's bugging you? Okay, the act wasn't marvellous, I can bear hearing it, Tommy, so tell me."

Of course, I was waiting for him to tell me my act was a knockout, because it wasn't bad, and I deserved a little spot in the show for it. Regularly.

"A knockout," he said. "It was a knockout." But his heart wasn't in it.

"Las Vegas, here I come," I said wryly.

"Your act was fine, kid. I always said you had it in you. You could go right to the top."

Now I *knew* something was up.

"I'm not knocking the club, Tom, but this is as far as I'll get."

He shook an admonitory finger at me.

"Don't underestimate yourself, Eddie, your moment of glory will come. Make no mistake."

"My moments of glory are all in my head, Tommy. What is it?"

He fiddled with a pile of fivers.

"How much do I pay you, kid?"

"Thirty."

"I'm giving you a bonus."

"What for?"

"What for nothing." He counted out some fivers and held them towards me. I didn't take them. He laid them on the edge of the desk in front of me. There was a pause as I looked at him and he looked away. With my fingers I spread out the fivers along the desk. There were twenty.

"A century. That's a bonus?"

"You did a good act, kid."

"I wish I'd seen it. What's the score, Tommy?"

There was a silence then he mumbled, "I want you to take a holiday."

"Where?"

"Anywhere."

"For how long?" He didn't reply, just shook his head and spread his hands. As I sat there, bewildered and hurt, he got up and, coming round his desk, scooped the money up and stuck it in the breast pocket of my tux.

"It's yours, Eddie."

I stood up, retrieved the money from my pocket, counted out six notes and put the rest on the table.

"My wages," I managed to say and turned for the door.

"Don't be like this, kid," Tommy pleaded to my back. I faced him from the door.

"Why? Just tell me why. It couldn't have been the act."

He shook his head again, "The act was fine."

"Then why?"

"Eddie. Someone doesn't like you. He can hurt people's businesses. Especially mine. In many ways."

"Who? I'll see him. Just tell me who."

He didn't answer. I opened the door.

"Anytime you want a favour, Eddie. Anything. Anytime."

"I don't want a favour, Tommy, just a job." I went out to use the pay 'phone to call a cab; somehow I didn't fancy getting the bus home that night. I can't remember being so sick inside since West Brom beat us 1-0 in extra time at Wembley in 1968. Any objective observer will tell you that that evening I had done a pretty fair act at the Broadway. I wasn't great and the gags were old, but I was better than many guys Tommy booked. And cheaper.

I had forgotten about asking Alison Wyatt to come to the flat to see me, and getting the boot from Tommy wasn't calculated to make me remember. I opened the door of the flat, put my hand out for the light switch and was picked up and thrown across the room. Then I remembered. Funny, I thought, a bit rough for a girl to behave. An unorthodox approach, if ever I saw one. I was pulled to my feet and the bedside lamp came on about an inch from my face, momentarily blinding me. The lamp was pulled back and between blinks I saw a guy of

77

about six four, holding the lamp in one hand and me in the other.

"Hello Alison, when did you have the operation?" I cracked, and he put the lamp on the bedside table and threw me back on the bed. If there'd been two more of me he'd have had a juggling act. He stooped over me and patted me for the rod, but I wasn't wearing it.

"You're the spade who was in the library."

"That's right."

"Listen, I'll take the books back and pay the fines," I smiled, but I was wishing I was up there and he was down here and I was about to do a José Greco on his face. Getting the sack was enough for anyone, getting done over the same evening was adding injury to insult.

"Stay where you are," he said, smiling. Then, in his best been-to accent, he repeated, "Stay where you are." (You heard of the been-to's? The African bourgeoisie who go to Europe for an education, go home and tell everyone where they've been. "Been to London," "Been to Paris," and so on. Been to Eddie Ginley's and did him over.)

"I know it's a bit late to ask, but you sure you got the right place?"

He looked me over. "These your working clothes, Mr Ginley?" he sneered.

I can sneer, too. "Don't they wear overalls where you come from?" I sneered back.

"Those are overalls?" he was still sneering.

"Don't you recognise a worker when you see him?" I was still sneering.

"You all look the same to me." He paused.

"You're an entertainer, aren't you?"

"A comic. You too, I believe. King Kong, isn't it?"

He said nothing.

"Godzilla, then?"

His hand snapped out, grabbed my wrist, and squeezed. I have to admit I yelped a bit.

"I could kill you," he said very, very quietly.

"Let go of my wrist, ape-man!" I warned, tearfully. He let go and I doubled over on the bed in agony, trying to massage some life back into my wrist. My arm was numb and my watch had stopped. This kid was strong. After a minute I looked up; he backed away, into the middle of the room. I stood up and glared angrily at him. There wasn't much else I could do.

"What were you doing with a gun, Ginley?"

"I use it in the act. It keeps the audience on its toes," I jumped nervously to one side as I expected him to come over. He didn't.

"You pulled the gun on Alison Wyatt in the library." Tell me something new.

"I heard she could tell jokes and I was trying to persuade her to join me in a double act." I jumped again, but he didn't move, and my confidence grew.

"I'm not amused, Ginley."

"Oh, no? Try this one. There was a guy with a queer parrot–" I moved too late, his hand slapped me hard on the face and my head ricocheted off the wall. I felt the blood surfing from my bottom lip. He thrust his face so close into mine that I couldn't put my hankie up to stop the bleeding.

"I'd rather talk, Ginley. Do you understand? Talk. If you want it the other way, very well. But I'd rather talk." He paused. "Today, in the library, I saw you with the gun. Alison told me you had money, too. What was it about? Did the fat man send you?"

Being angry makes you do stupid things. All I had to do was tell this guy I didn't know what the hell he was talking about, offer him the stuff, and add that I hoped that I never saw him or his bird, Alison Wyatt, ever again. So I said, "Okay, buster, you want answers? I'll give them to you. The gun's part of my job, see? Being a comic's only a front, I'm really a private eye. A girl, a grand and a gun. That's the world I move in, see? I know no fat man. If you want any more answers contact my solicitors, Messrs. Hill, Gott and Gains. And you're in my flat. Get out."

"That's your answer?"

"It's the only one you're going to get, now on your way, Mighty Joe Young."

He grabbed my trench lapels and pushed my head against the wall.

"Mr Ginley, I think you don't know anything at all. I think someone made a mistake and you're it."

He let go of me and I sagged. He walked to the door. He opened it, turned, and gave me a look, and, when he spoke, sounded oddly friendly and pathetic.

"Throw the gun away, Mr Ginley. Stick to entertaining. Stay out of what you don't know. Stay out of it."

I walked over to him, handkerchief to mouth. I looked at the blood on the handkerchief, then I looked at him.

"Tell me one thing, fellow," I said, "when did you come down from the trees?"

He smiled. "When I saw you crawl from under the stone."

"Well, you better get back among the bananas, then." I knew he had one hand on the door knob, because I could see it. It was the other hand, the one that punched me quick and hard into the stomach I didn't see. As I doubled over and sank to the floor in agony, I heard him quip, "You're the great white hope?" Then the door closed and he was gone.

It was some minutes before I could drag myself to the refrigerator and open the door. I pulled open the inner freezer door, took out the jumbo Birdseye pea packet and tipped it out on the fridge top. The gun, the money and the photo were still there. He hadn't searched the joint.

Later, as I walked home from the out-patients of the Royal (waited two hours for result of x-ray – us hypochondriacs take no chances), I knew I had only got what I deserved from the spade.

Much later I phoned a Mossley Hill number. A sleepy voice answered, "Hello?"

"Ellen. Get William out of bed."

"Eddie? Eddie, it's after midnight."

"Get him to the 'phone."

"Can't it wait until morning?"

"Get him up!" I barked at her.

"You sound upset."

"Damn right, baby. I want to speak to that schmok now."

"He's gone to London. What's the matter?"

81

"I got the boot at the club, that's what's the matter, and that's got to be my brother's doing."

"Don't be ridiculous, Eddie. Why would he do a thing like that?"

"Because he asked me to take my ad out of the paper and I refused."

"The detective ad?"

"What else?"

"Eddie, how could he? I *told* you he went to London tonight. Anyway, you misjudge him. He wouldn't be so vindictive."

"Listen, baby, you ever heard of the telephone? That's how he could do it. He wouldn't be so vindictive? He told my boss he'd ruin him if he kept me on. That's how vindictive he wouldn't be."

A silence.

"Eddie? You still there? Listen, I'm sorry you've been sacked but I'm sure William had nothing to do with it. Things will look better in the morning, I know."

"Get him off my back, Ellen. And keep him off." I'd fix him. Sure as hell. Some way.

"What are you going to do?" She sounded worried now.

"Gumshoe's the game, kid," and I put down the 'phone. Float like a butterfly, sting like a bee. That's me. When I fight at my own weight.

CHAPTER EIGHT

Someone undefined was thumping my head and shouting, "It's a knockout, Eddie! It's a knockout!" The thumping hurt my head, drummed in my ears and rose to a crescendo. I tried to stop the thumping, I turned and I twisted and put my arms over my head, but it still went on. Then it stopped; I opened my eyes, it was daylight and someone was thumping on my door. I shouted for them to shut up and tried to sit up. It was hard to do, my stomach hurt, and when I pulled up my T-shirt to look, I had bruise marks. He could hit, could that spade. I had better not wear a tight pair of jockeys today, the elastic would murder me, I thought as I struggled out of bed.

I opened the door an inch; a living doll stood there. Forty years old if she was a day, puffing at a foot long cigarette holder, but all the same, a living doll. I shoved the door to fast, leaped for my trench and quickly belted it on. I opened the door. She pushed past me into the room and stared snootily around. If I tell you she wore a fur coat you might get the idea she was one of those old biddies you see in the Wine Lodge, drinking to the memory of the girls who fell there during the war. She wasn't. It was a pretty swish piece of some fine animal's hide, dark brown, she was wearing.

Boots, black and highly polished.

Long, red hair, falling naturally on her shoulders. Large, brown eyes.

No make-up.

A big mouth. Ooh! I like big mouths.

She smiled. She had great choppers. I smiled back.

"May I come in?" she said.

"You're in."

"So I am." She flicked her ash on the floor. Cheeky, I thought. "You don't look well," she said.

"Wait till I put my teeth in."

She walked over to my bookshelves and started poking at the paperbacks with a long finger.

"You're from the Gas Board."

"No," she said, and shook her hair.

"The electricity? I'm sorry about the foreign coins in the meter, but I ran out of two bobs."

"I'm not from the electricity. Do I look as though I am?"

"I wouldn't know. I always try to be out when they come. The meter hasn't been emptied for months. There must be a fortune in it."

"Really?" She didn't sound interested.

I walked into my kitchen, sat down, and started on my cornflakes. I always set my cornflakes out before I go to bed. If I didn't, I'd never get a breakfast of any sort because I wouldn't bother in the mornings. I may be a bachelor, but that was no reason for not looking after myself.

I had my copy of Chandler's *The High Window* propped up against the milk bottle. I read a bit aloud from it, the bit where Breeze, the cop, shows Philip Marlowe the advert of George Anson Philips in the paper. Philips called himself a private eye, but no one agreed with him. I know how he felt. I read "Why worry? Why be doubtful and confused? Why be gnawed by suspicion? Consult cool, careful, confidential, discreet investigator. George Anson Philips. Glenview 9521."

She came into the kitchen. I stuffed some of Kellogg's best into my mouth and looked up at her. She was stubbing her fag out on my table. She blew down the holder to clear it from tobacco.

"Did you write that?" she asked.

"No."

"It sounds fascinating."

"It is fascinating."

"What's it called?"

"*The Plight of the Bumble Bee*. It's a book on ecology, how the insect's affected by pollution."

She looked at the cover. "It's called *The High Window*," she said. Quick as a flash. "Is it good?"

I put down my spoon.

"Lady. I've read it five times. This is the sixth. It helps me to plan my life. It's that good. And you've obviously got the wrong place, so why don't you leave me to my breakfast?"

She went and sat on my bed, crossed her legs, took a new fag from somewhere and lit it. She looked across at me and for a moment I thought she was going to cry. She was so sexy. I put down my spoon and stood up.

I walked across to the bed. Looked down at her.

"It won't work," I said.

"What won't work?" She looked up, her eyes so big I could have dived into them and swam about.

"This won't work. Oh! It'll be fine at first, you'll take me to the pictures. Box of chocolates. Necking in the back row with your hand on my leg and I'll have to stop you. Take me to dances, tell me how much you like being with me and hasn't anyone ever told me before how attractive I am. All the time trying to have your way with me and I'll be fighting you off. So what then? I give in. That's what. And I'll hang around the house every night waiting for you to call, but you won't. I'll walk down the block and they'll point their fingers and say 'There he goes. A box of chocolates, a few sweet words, and he's anybody's.' Then something'll happen that shouldn't happen, so where will I turn? You don't want me for myself. You want my body, that's all. You don't respect me. You just want your evil way. Well, I'm not that kind of a guy. I want a home, kids, the normal things. A wife who'll rush home from work at nights to be with me. I'm human. When I am cut, do I not bleed?" I stopped.

Give her her due; she didn't bat an eyelid.

"I'm looking for Ginley, the private investiga-

86

tor." She took a tightly rolled copy of the *Echo* out of her pocket. "I saw this ad in the paper so I came straight over."

I shook my head. "Sorry, the private investigator's out. I'm the comedian. What did you want with him?"

"You're the comedian?"

"Yes, ma'am."

"Was that stuff about taking you to the movies and chocolates and wanting respect a sample of your work?"

"Did you like it?" She did not reply.

"I have a job for Ginley," she said.

"What kind of a job?"

"A private investigating kind of job."

Ask a stupid question and you get a civil answer. I looked at her for a moment, then went back to my cornflakes; I pretended to read my book. She came into the kitchen.

"You wouldn't know where I could find him?" she appealed.

"For a private investigating kind of a job." It was a statement.

"That's what I said."

I shovelled the flakes down.

"Well?" she said.

"He wouldn't be interested," through the flakes.

"How do you know?"

"He told me so himself! 'Definitely no more investigating!' he said. It's wearing him out."

"You seem to know him awfully well." She stubbed the second fag out next to the first one on

87

the table. It's amazing what I'll stand for from beautiful women.

"He's like a brother to me," I said.

The 'phone rang.

"The 'phone."

"I heard, lady." I went across, picked it up and said "Call me back in five minutes. I'm in conference." There was a squawk on the line as I cradled the receiver.

"A friend?"

"My road manager. Okay, lady, just for the record, and just in case Ginley's interested, what's the job?"

"I'm being threatened." She started to look sad again.

"By whom?"

"A man."

"How is he threatening you?"

"I'm a widow." She spread her hands as though she were about to sink to the floor and beg forgiveness for it. "I'm a widow and this man who's threatening me was in business with my late husband. The nature of the business is not important, although I need hardly say that it was perfectly legal. He says that my late husband and I swindled him out of his share of the business. He says that we were three equal partners and that my late husband and I transferred the money the business made from the firm's account into my private account."

"And did you?"

"Certainly not! He was never a partner. He was an employee. A pretty useless employee at that.

Nobody else would have had him if we hadn't taken him into our firm."

"Tell him to push off."

"It's not as simple as that. I... I am about to be married," she said, like she was admitting to some perversion. "I am about to be married to an eminently respectable and wonderful person and this man threatens to reveal the swindle to my husband-to-be."

"The *alleged* swindle," I corrected.

"The alleged swindle?"

"Lady, if you say the swindle didn't take place and he says it did, then, until it's proved one way or the other, it's alleged."

"Of course. Anyway. I'm at my wits' end. I don't know what to do."

I felt for my fags in my trench coat and lit one. I drew in the smoke and had a coughing fit. Those Luckies can be pretty strong first thing in the day, even if you're prepared for them, even if you're an addict, like me.

I made for the kitchen roll on top of the fridge, tore off a strip, coughed up some catarrh into it, put it to my nose and blew into it, threw it in the bin and sat down.

"Tell the police," I said hoarsely.

"I couldn't. It would all come out. He wants money. It's blackmail, they'd prosecute."

"Then tell your husband-to-be about it."

"How could I do that?"

"You just said he was a wonderful person. If he wants to marry you he must love you. If there was no swindle like you said, he'll believe you."

"I couldn't. I'm scared. It's a very frightening business, blackmail."

"For someone who says she's scared, you look awfully cool to me."

"Appearances can be deceptive."

"Indeed they can, lady. Now you take this Ginley fellow you're looking for, the private eye guy. He looks very competent but he's really very stupid. For one, it may be very clear to *you* what your problem is, but to him it wouldn't. He'll wonder what the hell you wanted."

"I want this man stopped."

"What's he doing?"

"Phoning me."

"Change your number."

"I have. But I want him stopped. I want someone to warn him off."

"That sounds like a tough job."

"I pay very well."

I shook my head and tried lighting another fag. I didn't cough. I leaned back on my chair, and looked up at her.

"He's got a job."

"I'll double what he's getting now to come and work for me."

I shook my head again.

"He's that expensive?" she asked.

"He ain't expensive and he'd like to take the money, lady, but like I said, he has a job which he wants to see through."

"Can't he be bought at all?"

"Oh yes. He can be bought. But not with anything you've got, and not when he's doing

90

something else."

"Is that final?"

I toyed with the spoon in my cornflakes bowl.

She spoke very slowly. "Tell Mr Ginley he's being more stupid than he knows."

"I tell him all the time but he won't listen. Once he starts something he's got to finish it."

She walked to the door, opened it and turned.

"I'm sorry I wasted my time," she said, and went, leaving behind only the smell of her perfume and her cigarette butts on my table, which was sad. I didn't often get living dolls in my place, especially living dolls with posh voices. Especially with posh American voices.

The 'phone rang again.

"In conference with whom?"

"My road manager."

"Where's Danny?"

"I know that voice. It's Alison Wyatt. Who's Danny?"

"Danny Azinge. He went to your place last night." She started to cry.

"Godzilla? How should I know where he is? I don't like to broach an ugly new thought to you, but maybe he made it with someone else." She deserved *that*, the way her boyfriend treated me.

She didn't reply, just cried some more.

"Don't cry. Listen, meet me in my city office in half an hour."

"Where's that?" she managed to say through the sobs.

"75, Renshaw Street. Room 'A'. You can't miss it."

"You'll be there?" Anxious as hell.

"I'll be there, kid."

She rang off.

So. Danny Azinge was his name? And he didn't come home. So, some new chick struck lucky and Alison Wyatt didn't, it wasn't my problem. He wasn't sleeping in my bed. I'd make those points very strongly to her. You have to be cruel to be kind in those situations.

As for the living doll, I knew several things about her. She hadn't seen my address in the advert and come straight over like she said, because I hadn't put my address in it. And the job she offered was therefore a real phoney. There was something else. I could tell that straight off. I'm not dim. I may be green, but I'm no cabbage.

Down at the dole things moved slowly. Down at the dole things always move slowly. You will know that yourself, of course, if you have ever had to sign on; it's like another world. It *is* another world, too, for the unemployed. It's not the world they seem to know much about in Westminster, or care much about, either. "Three quarters of a million unemployed? That's terrible, we must do something about it, let's charge half a sheet for prescriptions. And while we are about it, let's really have a go at Social Security benefits for strikers. Let's stop them." "Good idea, Ted! Then there's school meals, milk subsidies, housing… there's no end to it really." You can get very worked up at the dole.

I sat on the commercial section waiting to give

the man in the cubicle the details I'd often given before.

I waited on the crowded bench, waiting to move to the next crowded bench, then to the crowded bench next to the cubicles where I'd wait to see the man. I moved up the bench as someone gave up waiting and went out.

Alison Wyatt sat next to me. Her eyes were red from crying. She started to sniff as I looked at her and I thought more tears were due. They weren't. I tried a grin. "You're late, Fats," I told her. She looked around.

"Why did you choose this place to meet?" she asked.

"One of those old proletarian customs, lady. You lose your job, you sign on at the dole."

She curled her lip at me. "*You* need a job? Yesterday you had a thousand pounds."

"That's in a numbered account."

"Switzerland, I suppose," she sneered.

"Co-op actually. You see, you can get it out on Saturdays then."

We sat silently for a few minutes. As silently as you can in the dole. People coughed, shuffled their feet, rustled newspapers, got up to walk about. The things everyone does while officialdom grinds tediously on.

She twisted a handkerchief round and round until her knuckles were white.

"Okay, Ginley, what have you done to Danny?"

"Danny as in Boy or Danny as in Kaye?"

"You know who I mean. Danny Azinge. He didn't come home when he went to see you."

"What was I supposed to have done with him? He'd make the Harlem Globetrotters look like Wee Georgie Wood."

Her voice was quiet, and sad, and despairing, saying, "He's disappeared. I'm asking you. You got him. What did you do with him?"

I felt as though I was talking to an extremely dim child, "Listen, after your friend, your extremely big and tough friend, finished trying to wallpaper the room with my brains, he left. I haven't see him since and if I never see him again it will be too soon."

"You had a gun," she persisted.

"We only met yesterday. For a couple of minutes. Even so I thought we understood each other." I put a hand on her arm. "It ain't my style, Fats. I may have had a gun, but it wasn't mine. Guns aren't me, you see."

She stood up, looked at me for a brief instant and, as the tears started to come, she turned and walked out. I watched her go. She stopped at the door. A man gave her a slip of paper and she went out. The man walked over to me and sat down. I shuffled along the bench as someone moved to the next bench. The man looked at me, smiled, and held out his hand. I shook it. It seemed to be the thing to do at the time.

"John Straker," he said.

"Eddie Ginley."

"Pleased to meet you, Eddie."

"Likewise."

He took a packet from his pocket. "Would you like a Polo?" he said.

"No thanks. My dentist says mints rot your teeth."

He pointed to his mouth. "Dentures."

"Lucky you," I said.

"I'm Scottish," he said, "from Glasgow."

"Your accent gave you away," I told him.

"I'm Jewish, too."

"Some people get all the breaks."

"I like you." He smiled again. I looked him over. A short man. About forty. A neat blue suit, dark tie, a trilby hat with a small brim and a coloured hatband. Long grey sideboards. A Zapata moustache. All very dapper. Sauchiehall Street Smoothie. He took off his hat, put it on his knee and laid the packet of mints inside it.

"You a friend of Alison's?" I asked.

"In a manner of speaking, Eddie. In a manner of speaking."

"What did she mean?"

"You mustn't be too hard on her, lad. She liked you. She took a lot of convincing that you'd grabbed her boyfriend."

"I'd take a lot of convincing on that score, too."

"I know lad, it's ridiculous."

We moved on to the next bench. He sat very close.

"You gave her something?"

"Yes, lad. An address where she can rejoin her boyfriend."

I looked at him; his face seemed vaguely familiar now I'd come to look at it.

"I know you, Jock."

"*John*, Eddie, the name's *John*. I think I may have

95

seen you at the hotel. There was a bit of a mix-up there. You were a very naughty laddie."

"Listen, I don't know what the hell this is all about."

"That's the way to keep it, Eddie."

"What do you want me for?"

"I don't want you at all, lad."

We moved up a bench again. Three more people to go and it was my turn for the cubicle.

"I don't want you at all, lad," he repeated. "I just want the money. I don't want the black lad, Azinge. I wanted the girl, and I've got her, and I want the money, and you've got that. That's all. So be a good lad and hand it over."

"I don't know what you are talking about."

He shook his head and smiled wearily. "Eddie, don't be dim," he said. He looked around. "You know, I haven't been in a Labour Exchange for years. It's a funny feeling."

"Cut the reminiscence, Angus."

"They said you were a comic, Eddie. Save it!"

We shuffled up the bench. He took the Polos out of his hat and offered them.

"You sure you won't have one? They're wonderful for concentration."

"They help you to think about where your teeth went, do they?"

"I said save it, Eddie." He paused. "You know, you've come to the right place."

"Clue me in."

"Because you're going to need the money they give you. You're going to be a thousand pounds lighter after this morning. You did me a lot of harm when you picked up that packet from the Exchange. I don't like that."

"I'll split it with you. Half each."

He shook his head, "Son, it's not just the money. If it was, I wouldn't mind. It's my reputation that's at stake. I couldn't hold up my head if an amateur like you hustled me out of a job. And you nearly did that, lad, when you picked up the package. It was not very nice, you know."

He looked at me as though I'd hurt him badly.

"You're a very sensitive guy, John."

"Where's the money?"

"At my place."

"Let's go and get it."

I nodded to the cubicle. It was my turn next.

"Mind if I see a man about a job?"

"Sure lad, sure. I've been in the same boat myself. But make it quick."

The bell from the cubicle tinkled. I started to get up and Straker's fingers bit into my arm.

"No tricks lad. Be sensible. I'm a hard man. I may not look it, but I am. I hurt people who upset me. Don't upset me, Eddie, or I'll hurt you. I really will. Believe me."

"I believe you, I believe," I protested. I did too. He let go of my arm and I got up, went into the cubicle and sat down.

"Hello Eddie," the clerk said, smiling.

I looked at him. Everyone knew me and I did not know them.

"You don't remember me, do you? Phil Hoadley. We were at school together. You were a year lower than me."

We shook hands.

"Of course I remember you. How are you going, Phil?" I didn't remember.

"Not bad. You?"

"Not bad."

"I saw an ad in the paper the other day. It was you, wasn't it? As soon as I saw it, I said to the wife, 'I used to go to school with him.' And there you were, touting for work in the *Echo*. You're not losing faith in us, are you?"

"No."

"That's a good lad."

"You couldn't do us a favour, could you?"

"What is it?"

I leaned conspiratorially across the counter.

"A guy out there. I owe him some money. He's getting nasty."

"Bum Bailiff, is he? How much do you need?" He reached into his inside pocket.

"Too much for you, Phil. I just want to avoid him."

"Taking it on the lam, are you?" he grinned.

"You got it, Phil."

He looked at me seriously for a moment.

"It's against regulations, Eddie."

"Break them just this once," I begged.

"If it was to come out that I let you through…" He shook his head.

"I don't even know you."

He pondered, then, "For you, Eddie, be my guest."

I slithered over the desk like a snake and crouched down beside his chair.

"Keep going – don't let anyone stop you," he warned, "and here," he thrust a file of papers into my hand, "tell them you're from the Mersey Docks and Harbour Board. That sounds impressive."

I took the file.

"If you stand up and stoop you can't be seen from out there," he said. I did so.

"Thanks a million, Phil."

"Gumshoe's the game, eh Eddie?" he grinned, and I was off.

I pushed through a partition door behind Phil's desk and Quasimodoed my way past a row of desks with girls working at them, to a doorway. The girl at the last desk looked up at me. I put the file on her desk. "Check this," I told her. She took it. I went through the doorway. Facing me was a staircase. I went up it and found myself in a gallery that ran round the whole of the room. When I looked down I could see the benches, and Straker sitting where I left him. I could see Phil tinkle his bell and Straker darting up because that meant the cubicle was empty. I started round the gallery to the far staircase as Straker began to pull Phil across the desk. Some day I'd have to buy Phil a drink, I thought as I ran down the stairs, if I could avoid Rob Roy down there. I pushed open a door. I was in an alley. At the top of the alley I could see the road, and traffic. I didn't hesitate. I legged it. I was away. The breaks seemed to be going my way.

They weren't.

I had to find a 'phone box and make a call.

The Lotus Europa pulled up at the end of the platform. It was a nice looking heap. The fastest bread vans on wheels, Arthur called them.

Ellen got out and looked around for me. I signalled to her from the archway where I stood. She came across.

She didn't look very happy.

"You got the package?"

"Here." She shoved it at me. I put it in my pocket.

"I don't want to know, Eddie," she rasped.

"What's wrong, love?"

"Don't 'love' me. I don't want to be included in your games."

She worried me. I tried a grin.

"Was it something I said?"

"Why did you make me pick the package up from your flat?" She was still rasping.

"It's a long tale, kid."

"It's a short story, Eddie," she snapped. "There was a man there."

"In the flat? A Scots fellow? How did he let you walk out with the package? What did he say?"

"He didn't say anything. He was dead."

I fell back against the wall. I needed the support.

"Dead? Straker?"

"How am I supposed to know his name. All I saw was that he was black and that he was dead."

"Azinge."

The whistle went.

"You'd better get on your train."

"Sure," I said dumbly.

"So long, Eddie." She turned and walked away.

100

I got on the train, went into one of the lavatories and locked the door. I pulled the lid down, sat on the seat and thought. I needed more time, I needed a lot more speed. What I didn't need was a body in my flat. What I had to do was to break this case, but fast. Before it broke me. Before someone broke me. I pulled out the package. Everything was still in it. I took out the gun and put it in my trench pocket. I lifted the flap of brown paper. There was the label, "Atlantis Books, Museum Street, W.C.1." Someone down there had to know what it was all about. They had to.

So why not go to the police? A decent, law-abiding citizen who finds himself in a jam, who has evidence that a crime has been committed, should head straight for the boys in blue and tell all. They will understand. They will put things right. No matter that the evidence you have of a crime committed is that a reliable eye witness saw a dead body in your flat. He could have cooled naturally, of course, it has been known. It just wasn't likely. Not with the company I'd been keeping.

"There's a body in my flat, officer."

"Is that B-O-D-Y, sir?"

"His name's Azinge. I think he was murdered by a Scotsman named Straker. I don't know how because I haven't been back to see."

"I see, sir. A body in your flat."

"There's also a matter of this money, this photograph of a girl, and this .38 Smith & Wesson. I got them at the Exchange Hotel. It was a mistake. They were meant for the Scots fellow. But that's funny too, because I was 'phoned up to collect them, although I thought it was a gag… You see, officer, someone meant to queer the pitch for Straker… it's very hard to explain."

"Wesson, sir. Now is that two esses?"

It would be very hard to explain. Very hard.

It would be very hard if coppers were nice. And they're not. You never go to coppers with your troubles. Unless you want more trouble.

My old man used to say that you could only tell the difference between coppers and villains because one lot wore uniforms; except when they were in plain clothes.

Sure, if your child gets molested, if you get burgled, if you see a runaway horse, call the police.

Not all policemen are the same, of course. Somewhere, in some little village there must be a copper who says "Evenin' all. A funny thing happened on my patch last night…" Somewhere there may be Charlie Barlows and John Watts keeping the community free from crime, and an 87th Precinct where the police are ordinary joes who happen to find themselves knee-deep in the eight balls trying to keep society working. Somewhere, there are good coppers.

Ask anyone with long hair about policemen.

Ask any spade who lives in Notting Hill about policemen.

Ask *any* spade anywhere.

Ask any demonstrator about policemen.

Ask anyone who's been involved in an unofficial strike about policemen. Ask them about those funny fellows with cloth caps, mufflers, big boots,

102

cameras and note-books who appear at meetings.

Ask anyone left of Harold Wilson. There's quite a few of us.

Chicago, 1968. Democratic Convention. Remember?

It's rumoured that a guy walked into a bank, smack dab in the middle of Mayor Daley's patch, took out a gun and said to one of the tellers, "Hand over the money, or I'll send for the police." No kidding.

There must be some good coppers.

Somewhere.

I don't know any.

CHAPTER NINE

I hoisted the A to D on top of the pay 'phone and looked up the Atlantis Bookshop. It wasn't hard to find. I was there inside twenty minutes from Euston.

It stood at the end of a small street, running down from the British Museum, in between two cafés. I pretended to look in the window of a shop opposite specialising in copies of Roman and Greek antiquities, every so often sneaking a glance across the road to the Atlantis. I was working up the courage to go in. I didn't know what I was looking for, who I was looking for. All I had to go on was a label from the package I got at the hotel. It could have been coincidence the label was there. The guy wrapping the package could have used any old piece of brown paper. He need not have any connection with the shop.

It could have, though.

There could be somebody there who would take me apart. Like the man said, it was a chance I had to take.

I walked across the street.

I was a long way from home, friends and family. You could keep the family but I was a long way from the other two.

I snatched a look in the window before I went in. Books on the occult, tomes on witchcraft, magic, packs of tarot cards and a silver dagger made up the display. By the door was an old card table piled with crime paperbacks and "Teach Yourself" books. There wasn't one called *Teach Yourself Detection*. I went in.

Just inside the door someone sat reading a book behind an L-shaped arrangement of two small tables. I say 'someone' because long hair fell forward almost obscuring the book, so I couldn't determine the sex of the person I figured to be the proprietor. He or she didn't look up.

In the centre of the shop was a large, squarish sort of table displaying occult periodicals. At the back, to the left, was a staircase that led down to some sort of basement, I supposed. The rest was shelves of books, divided into alcoves on the left side of the shop, a wall of books on the other. There was only one other customer, a tall old party in a khaki canvas riding coat, looking at the stuff across the display table from me. I pulled out a book. It was about werewolves. I was leafing through it wondering whether to get William a copy, when I looked up to see a pair of bright blue eyes glittering at me. The old party. His face was like a shiny red apple someone had pinched into the twin peaks of nose and chin. He shut one of his eyes slowly in a wink, then the pinched-apple face was suddenly split by a huge grin, exposing two large, white teeth. The grin and the wink over, the man pointed to the shelves behind him and commenced stuffing books into the voluminous inside pockets of his mac. Then, as much as he could under the weight of the books, he straightened up, gave me the thumbs-up sign and another wink and lumbered out of the shop, belting his mackintosh.

The person at the desk looked up from reading the book. The 'person' was a very pretty girl of about twenty-two or so, with a very pale face and large, fine grey eyes. She watched the old guy go and looked across at me.

"He thinks I don't notice, you know," she said.

"Why don't you stop him?"

"Because it gives him a thrill to think he's a brilliant shop-lifter."

"You must lose plenty."

She shook her head. "I just make out a list of the books he's taken and send the bill to his mother."

"He's got a mother?"

"Haven't we all?" she grinned.

She leaned back in her chair and played with the thin gold chain at her throat that held a Magen David.

"You can stop pretending now," she said.

"Come again," I said.

"These books aren't for you. You're not the type." She grinned again. She had a beautiful grin.

It's not often that pretty girls bother to give me the time of day, never mind grin, so I took the opportunity to walk across to the desk and pursue the matter. What would she know about guns, hoods threatening you in the dole and dead bodies. I was beginning to feel better already. I leaned on the desk.

"There's a definite type, is there?" I asked.

"Not what you'd think. No black cloak and broomstick stuff. The most respectable people buy the occult."

She leaned forward on the desk. She was wearing a good perfume.

"I could tell when you walked into the shop that you weren't here to buy a book, that you weren't idly browsing, that you weren't a tourist." She counted the kinds of people I wasn't on the fingers of one hand. "Aren't I clever?"

"Very." I gestured round the shop. "What do you think of this... er... merchandise you're selling? You believe it all?"

She looked at the shelves. "The books? It's all crap. Crap. It's a load of crap. I'm in the crap business."

What you might call a positive response.

"That's what I think, too."

I took out a pack of Luckies and offered her one. She took it. I lit both cigarettes. She leaned back again.

"You own this place?"

She shook her head. "He's out buying. You want to see him?"

"When will he be back?"

"Couple of hours, three maybe, why?"

"Why what?"

"Why would a nice-looking guy like you want to see him?"

That doesn't happen often either, with pretty girls.

"Thank you, I'm flattered," I said.

"You haven't answered."

"Business."

She looked at me and nodded. "I see."

"You see what?"

"I could also tell when you came into the shop you were looking for something. The word's got round has it?"

"I don't follow." I didn't.

"You don't need the stuff. I can tell you."

"Stuff?"

She threw her hands into the air. "Okay. Be cagey. Do I care?" .

I was mystified; I moved to the door. "Back in three hours, right?"

"That's what I said," she said.

"Tell me something."

"Anything. I'm twenty-three. Unmarried. A lot of time on my hands."

I grinned at her. "This guy who owns the shop. Is he a mate or just a boss?"

"Lawrence? He's a creep, he just pays my wage. He's just The Man. You dig?"

I dug. A girl after my own heart.

"Do us a favour. Don't tell him I called," I said.

"I wouldn't tell him how high was up," she said.

109

"What's your name?"

"Naomi. Yours?"

"Eddie."

"Call again, Eddie."

"I will."

"Any evening after six."

"Is that when you knock off?"

"Yes. It's also when I blossom."

I grinned again – I felt I could afford to – and left the shop.

I had three hours to kill and not much idea how to kill them. This was only my third time in London and the other two times I had been there were day trips to see Cup Finals. I didn't want to go to a movie. Afternoons were not my times for seeing films because for some reason I always felt guilty when I came out. Still do, for that matter.

Also, the police might be looking for me. If Straker had put a cadaver in my flat he was certainly up to telling the police about it and set them to looking for me.

I went into the café next door to the bookshop and drank my way through half a dozen cups of coffee as the time ticked away. I sat next to the window to see who came and went from the bookstore.

I had lit what seemed like my three hundredth Lucky and started on my seventh cup of coffee when I looked up and saw a face looking in at me from the window. A large round face that was partly obscured by a giant pair of shades. A face that belonged to a short, thickset frame, covered as

110

far as I could see by a donkey jacket. The face vanished from the window and seconds later appeared at the door of the café. He came in, hands deep in the pockets of the donkey jacket, and sat opposite me. He leaned across the table and spoke in an intense whisper.

"Let's talk very naturally."

"We can if you stop whispering," I said.

"Don't try to be funny," he continued. "Just answer my questions. I've a gun under the table. I'd hate to use it. Okay? So let's look like we're old pals. Don't try anything. I've got a guy in the street and one out back, if you do."

"What do you want?"

He didn't reply so I leaned across the table and removed his sunglasses.

"I haven't had them off since Buddy Holly died," he grinned, sheepishly.

"How do you wash, then?" I asked him.

"Inadvertently."

"Mal Evans!"

"Eddie Ginley!"

We sat there grinning at each other in that daft way mates who haven't seen each other in years do.

"Bum!" I told him.

"Bum yourself!" he laughed. "Jerry Lee Lewis!" he cried.

"Little Richard!"

"Elvis Presley!"

"78's."

"You playing them all night at our house and driving me mam mad," he laughed.

And I laughed. Laughing together in the warm

111

glow of good times remembered between two late developing ex-teddy boys.

"How long you been down here, Mal?"

"Five years," he said, as if apologising.

"Why did you come?"

"Me mother sold me guitar," he said. "Sold her kid's guitar, eh?" He laughed. "Well. I was twenty-five." We did some more grinning at each other.

"You living here, Eddie?"

"On a visit."

"Did you ever marry that bird of yours? What was her name?"

"Ellen. No, I didn't. You?"

"Married? Yeah. Look at this." He produced some little boxes and put them on the table. "Dinky cars."

"Do you collect them?"

He shook his head. "For my lad," he said proudly.

"You got a son?"

"Two months old. I'm laying in a stock for when he's older. All the things I never had, he's getting."

"Starting with Dinkies?"

"Starting with Dinkies."

"Do you want a coffee?"

"No thanks, Eddie, I've got to go in a minute." He looked at me. "Do you think they'll ever invent a time machine?"

"What for?"

"I'd like to go back for my guitar. Give that to my lad, too," and he laughed.

We fell to silence. That kind of embarrassed silence old mates. who've never met in years, feel when they realise they've gone different ways. When, because they've gone different ways, there's not much more to talk about after they've talked about old times.

"Look us up someday," Mal said.

"Sure," I told him.

"We're in the book."

"Great."

He got up to go, scraping his toy cars into his pocket. He put on his shades and held out his hand as though asking for money.

"Put it there, kid," he grinned. I slapped the outstretched palm.

"Hang loose, Big Bopper," I said, an old gag between us.

He went. Outside, he stuck his palm flat on the window. I covered it with mine. Then he was gone.

I had more coffee.

I made a pyramid of the cups.

I smoked through a whole pack of Luckies.

I went out and bought the two London evening newspapers, but there was no news of a nation-wide search for me.

I switched to tea and had two cups.

It was time to see what was going in the Atlantis bookshop.

It was dusk now and the lights were on in the shop. The salesgirl had gone, to blossom elsewhere, presumably. There didn't seem to be anybody in the place. I tried the door. It was locked. I looked up and down the street. It was still. I rapped on the door and waited. Nobody came.

113

The proprietor of the café where I had swilled in coffee came out and locked his door and went home. I waited until he had gone, then took out the Smith and Wesson and banged on the bookshop glass as loudly as I could without breaking it. A few moments later a head appeared at the top of the stairwell at the back of the shop. I held the gun to my side. A seedy-looking individual with a pasty face came to the door. He had a shock of black hair, National Health-style specs and was dressed in an old fireman's overcoat.

He mouthed "We're closed" at me and turned to go. I pressed my folded dole card against the glass. He looked at it, unlatched the chain and opened the door a couple of inches.

"What do you want?" he said, in a very narked whine. "Police, is it?"

"Yes. Let me in."

He stepped back as I pushed my way into the shop and flattened myself against the door. His eyes blinked nervously behind the spectacles.

"Here. You don't look like the law," he quavered.

I snapped, "This is law enough, fellow," and I jerked the .38 up at him.

He stared in horror at the gun and for a second or two I thought he was going to pass out.

"I've only books here," he babbled, "no money. Only books. Occult books – no novels."

I stuck the gun in his face. "Shut up." He shut up. "Who's downstairs?"

"No-one. I'm here alone," he said in a strangled voice. I pushed him to the back of the shop.

"Move!" I told him, but it was unnecessary because he was moving.

I poked him downstairs with the gun and at the bottom I grabbed him by the shoulder.

"What's to the left?"

"Toilet and washroom, but–"

"Shut up!" There was a door to the right. "Where does that go to?"

"The fire escape and to the street at the back." I pointed to the door ahead. "That?"

"My office and storeroom."

"Get in." I pushed him. He went stumbling through the door and I waited for someone else to appear, but nobody did.

He stood shaking in the middle of a room that looked like a bookshop in itself. There was a desk in the corner.

"You're Lawrence, right?" He nodded his head in agreement. Looking at him from the doorway I suddenly realised that despite his pasty face and his general seedy aspect he was at least six feet tall which made him a lot bigger than my five seven, and that alone was enough to take care of a gun-less Ginley, or a gun-ful Ginley if he wanted. I'm chicken from way back, really. If this guy knew nothing about the package and got nasty, I'd be the loser of the decade, I thought.

"Sit down," I ordered, and he sat behind the desk in the corner. It had a table lamp on it with a shade you could swivel. I switched it on and shone the light on his face. I was full of ideas. Very carefully, watching him all the time, I pulled the package out of my pocket and put it on the desk.

"Look at it."

He looked.

"See the label on it?"

He nodded.

"It's your label."

"Yes," he murmured, still scared.

"I got that package in Liverpool. How did it get there?"

He looked at me nervously. "Did you buy it?"

"Did I buy it?"

He tried a grin. "You know. With money."

I leaned across the table and grabbed him by the sweater and gave him a nostrilful of the .38. I think I also gave him ulcers. He definitely wasn't enjoying the experience. Neither was I.

"What would be in the package if I bought it?"

"A book?" he was asking me.

"If it wasn't a book, what would it be?"

He didn't reply for a moment, so I pulled harder on his sweater.

"It would be a package," he croaked fearfully.

"A package with a package inside? Of what? A package of what?"

"Stuff," he said.

"What stuff?"

"You're not the law are you? The law don't carry guns. I could see you weren't the law by the gun," he babbled.

"You're a bright fellow, Lawrence. Now what *stuff*?"

"What was that card you showed me, if you aren't the law?"

"My dole card. Now what *stuff*?" There wasn't

116

much more I could do with the gun except try and stick it right up his nose.

"I can get you some stuff if you want it." Realisation came late, but it came.

"Drugs?" I said.

"You didn't know?"

"No."

"Honestly?" He was amazed.

"Honestly. What kind of drugs?"

"That would be telling," he said coyly, as if the threat had now passed.

"If you think I won't use this gun you'd better think again," I said.

"Heroin. It's pretty good stuff. I can get you some if you like."

"Who do you send it to in Liverpool?"

He seemed to sense now that I really *wouldn't* use the gun. He could see I was no hardcase.

"Find out," he sneered.

I pulled back the hammer and cocked the gun. The words came out of his mouth in a rush.

"I don't know his name, I just send them express to Lime Street Station. The Red Star service. Whoever it is picks it up there. I just address the package 'Atlantis, care of the station'. They send the money here, in cash, before I send the stuff."

"Isn't that risky?"

"It's so risky, it's safe. It's ridiculously safe," he boasted.

"When are you sending the next lot?"

"I've just come back from the station – I sent it–" he stopped. He knew he'd goofed.

117

I let go of his sweater and he stared at me malevolently.

"You don't know who picks the stuff up in Liverpool?"

Before he could reply there was a sound from the shop upstairs. He heard it too.

"Who would that be?" I hissed.

"Nobody. Unless you got friends."

I switched the table lamp off and the overhead light. I stood behind the door motioning him to silence with the gun. The stairs creaked. I could feel my palm sweating against the stock of the gun. I didn't relish holding two men with the peacemaker; my nerves wouldn't be able to take it. I also didn't relish the idea of zapping whoever it was coming down the stairs, with the barrel of a .38. I read where you could kill people that way. It wasn't like in the movies where people fell over when you hit them and got up with no ill effects.

There was a chair on the other side of the door. I pocketed the gun and leaned across for it, making a hard face at Lawrence. He was as scared as I was. It looked like he had a shop full of hoods.

The figure of a man was silhouetted against the glass of the door. The figure of a man about my size, wearing a hat. The door creaked open.

What happened then is what I like to think of now as my plan. At the time I thought it was simply fear. Because I moaned.

I moaned aloud.

The door pushed open, the man came through the door and I bashed him across the legs with the chair. He fell with a cry of pain as I leapt across him

118

and made for the door that led to the back way out.
I jerked it open and was off, up an alleyway to freedom. It seemed like I was always making my bid
for liberty in alleyways. There were some stone
steps ahead that led onto the street. As I mounted
them I heard footsteps pounding along behind me.
Either he had legs like iron or I hadn't hit him hard
enough.

I made the pavement and ran across the road in
front of a lot of inconsiderate traffic whose brakes
squealed and whose horns blared at me. So this
was Bloomsbury? Haunt of Virginia Woolf, Lytton
Strachey? Didn't they call themselves the
Bloomsbury Group? Who played bass guitar and
did the vocals? You think some funny things when
you're running for your life. My psychiatrist says I
have an unnatural flippancy about life. Maybe he's
right. I ran down a short street to where a main
road crossed it. There was a bus pulling to a stop. I
threaded my way through more discourteous traffic and leapt on the platform as it started to move.

I sank onto one of the long seats, gasping for
breath. The bus stopped for some traffic lights.
Someone else bundled onto it. My pursuer. A very
annoyed, a very out-of-breath pursuer. The
Scottish, Jewish hood from the dole, Straker. My
Yiddisher momser. He pulled himself onto the seat
opposite, heaving up his lungs and trying to rub
his legs.

"You hurt my legs," he said, with great difficulty.

"Hard luck," I said with equal difficulty.

"I lost my hat, running," he gasped.

119

"You're breaking my heart," I gasped back. Then, when I had recovered my breath:

"Are you going to write to Alf Ramsay or shall I?"

"What do you mean?" he said.

"To tell him not to consider us for Munich in 1974. We're not fit now, we'd never make it for then."

He glared at me as the conductor came downstairs, demanding "Fares, please."

"He's got them," I said, indicating Straker, leaving him cursing, struggling for his money as the bus drew to a stop and I jumped off. I bashed my way through the people on the pavement and went down into Leicester Square Station.

I didn't bother with buying a ticket, just went through the barrier and took the escalator steps two at a time, going down.

There was no train in as I arrived on the platform puffing, but there was Straker right behind me. He could have given Jimmy Johnstone of Celtic lessons in speed, that fellow.

I hung back as the train came in, waiting until everyone had got on. Waiting until the doors were closing to make my move. I squeezed through the doors as they slid closed. The train moved as I sat down. Straker came up the carriage and sat next to me. He really was fast. Oh, Lord, if you can't help me then please don't help this haggis.

"I thought I had you there, John."

"You have to be quicker than that, Eddie," he said. "I was waiting for that move."

"You've been training, have you?"

120

"I told you I'm a pro, Eddie. A pro."

"You couldn't play for England, though," I said. "I've had second thoughts. You're Scots. You'd have to play for Scotland."

"Stop wittering, lad," he said wearily.

"Okay, I'll stop wittering if you tell me why you stuck that spade in my flat."

He gave me a puzzled look. "Come again?" he said.

"The spade in my flat. Dead. You put him there. Why?"

"Good God, man! Are you serious?" he cried.

"Come on, Straker. You put him there. Now why? You had the girl and you wanted the money, but did you have to kill Azinge?"

"I swear, Eddie, I swear I know nothing about the black lad. Other than I told the girl he was okay, and sent her off to rejoin him, I know nothing about it. They wanted her, Eddie. Not the blackie. Not you. Just her."

"Who are 'they'?"

"Give me the money, lad."

"Who are 'they'?" I persisted.

"They must have taken you horning in on this harder than me, lad. They're out to fix you. I'm professional, like I said. Like I told you; I hurt people who hurt me, but I do it *my* way. I fix people *direct*, I wouldn't fix you by planting a stiff on you, I'm not taking responsibility for what they do, Eddie. They're not professional. Now give me the money. I'll go away. Just give me the money and I'll go."

"I'd like to believe that."

121

"You never bloody listen!" he shouted, then went crimson as people turned round to stare at us. He grabbed my arm. "I've been trying to tell you," he said thickly, "I've not been paid for you. Only for the girl. I got the girl, now I want the money."

"Just like any other job," I said.

"A thousand before, a thousand after," he said.

"A job. A few potatoes to earn. Like the next guy."

"You make a living. They give you a name, you do your job and get paid. It's no-one you know. It's impersonal."

"It's not impersonal now."

"It's been a long day for both of us, Eddie."

"I said it's not impersonal now."

"I know it isn't," he agreed, "I know you now. I wouldn't enjoy knocking you off, but I'd do it all the same, lad, impersonal or not."

He shoved something hard into my side under the armrest of the seat. I couldn't see what it was because he had his hand in his pocket, but it didn't take much imagination to guess.

"What a way to make a living," I said.

"I get by."

"Get by without me."

He looked at me with a sort of tired sympathy. "What's in this for you, Eddie? Why did you turn up at the hotel? Why are you being so obtuse?" He genuinely wanted to know.

I gave him a friendly smile. "The curse of the Ginleys. We never know when we're licked," I said.

122

"Who put you up to going to the hotel, lad?"

"I don't know, but I aim to find out. What do they want with the girl?"

"Who knows, lad?"

"How did you get into this work, John?"

He smiled, "It's a cliché, lad."

"Tell me."

"Well, you're poor, you can't box or play football, so what else do you do? Also, you live in Glasgow, you're not Protestant or Catholic, so you either grow up fighting or go down for the count."

"That's very sad."

"Don't take it to heart, lad, it happens to millions."

"Tell me something."

"Okay. Then give me the money."

"Right."

"What is it?" he said.

"Will you take your bloody hand off my leg?" I shouted and leapt up. "You bloody queers, disgusting it is!" I addressed the passengers in the train who were staring at a horrified Straker. "He's been following me all night. I don't know, you come to London for the day. Sightseeing. The Tower, Buckingham Palace, the Changing of the Guard, and what happens?" The train pulled into a station, "You get people like him. Hands everywhere. It's disgusting. It won't stop here, you know. We'll be inundated with them if we're not careful. We've got to make a stand!" The doors opened. Straker was riveted to his seat. "I'm writing to my M.P. !" I shouted and slid between the closing doors onto the platform. I had a fine close-

123

up of Straker at the window, shouting something doubtless unprintable, as the train moved off.

I started as I felt a hand on my shoulder. I looked up.

"Come on, chief, we've been in ten minutes," said the porter. I swung my legs off the seat and sat up. I got off the train.

Cold, grey, 6 a.m. Lime Street. I went to the Red Star parcels office, bought a paper, bundled myself into a cab and gave the Mossley Hill address. I didn't really need the paper. The porter had got a good look at me, so had the ticket collector, the man at Red Star, the newspaper seller, the cabby. They had all the time in the world to look. I was the only non-railwayman about at the time in the station. Nobody had shouted. Nobody had screamed. No headlines in the *Daily Post* reading 'Police seek comedian to help in Enquiries. Student dead.' The cooled Azinge obviously wasn't hot.

A window was open. I got in easily. I made a pot of tea, poured a cup and sat down to wait. I didn't wait long. William appeared in the kitchen doorway. In a silk dressing gown over silk pyjamas. Holding a gun. He wasn't pleased.

I held up the teapot. "Shall I be mother, brother?" I poured a cup. William's face was working away but no sound was coming out yet. I held up the bowl. "Sugar or bile beans?"

He put the gun on the table, saying, with as much control as he could muster, "What the hell is this?"

124

I looked up at him in feigned surprise. "Tea, of course."

"I'm in no mood, Eddie."

"Mood for what?" I picked up the gun. "You shouldn't carry this around the house, Bill. Save it for conducting your business practices."

"I'm calling the police."

"Do that, Billy."

I played with the gun. It was a Webley air pistol, you could probably hit a stationary bus with it, at three feet.

"You pack a mean rod, Sheriff," I told him.

He looked at me malevolently. "No wonder you're seeing a psychiatrist," he spat out. "I'm amazed he hasn't certified you and locked you away."

I jumped up and pulled out the .38. He jerked back in fright. "Now you can treat me as an equal, William. Get your wife down here."

He went to the door and called "Ellen!" in a strangled voice.

"Project, brother, project!"

"Ellen!" he shouted.

"Sit down," I ordered. He came back and sat at the table. He fished his cigarettes and lighter from his pocket. He lit one without offering them and Ellen appeared at the doorway. She was dressed like William, a dressing gown over men's pyjamas, but she looked a lot fresher than he did. She looked like it happened every day of the week that people broke into the house and waved guns at her husband. Maybe I'm making her out to be cooler than she looked. After all, I was her brother-in-law.

125

She sat at the table, next to William; the Bisto Kids.

"Hello, Eddie, how have you been keeping?" As though she hadn't seen me in years.

"Been keeping the pot warm for baby. Pour yourself a cup."

She did.

"Okay, Billy, you got me the sack from the club."

"You wouldn't take the advert out of the paper. I warned you," he sneered.

"What do you do if someone treads on your toes on the bus, Billy? Have his feet amputated?"

"I never travel on the bus." Quick as a flash. Brotherly repartee again, you see.

I looked at Ellen. "He wouldn't be that vindictive, eh, kid?"

She said nothing.

"Okay, William, now I'll tell you a tale that will make even your piggy eyes pop." I paused to give him time to get his ugly look working again. "Ellen here, dear old Ellen, waves me off to London with the news that there's a body in my flat."

He looked at me coolly.

"Your piggy eyes ain't popping, Bill."

"She told me," he said.

"What wife wouldn't? You'd sell cancer to a dying man, William, but I don't think you'd plant a stiff on your brother. It wouldn't look good for the Ginley name. A dead man in my modest stash – imagine my mortification. No joke intended, of course. You see the jam I'm in?"

"I don't see that you're in a jam," he said.

126

"Really? But you see, William, leaving aside the corpse a minute, when I got to London someone tried to knock me off."

"He'll have to take his place in the queue," he said.

"The point is, only Ellen knew I was going to London. How about that?"

He shot her a glance. She sipped her tea, unconcernedly. "I don't know what you're talking about, Eddie," she said between sips. "I'm just the messenger boy, remember? I do the dirty work, you're the gumshoe."

"There's an awful presumption there, Ellen. Like I sent you to the flat knowing the body was there. It ain't true, kid."

I got up to go.

"Sit down, Eddie," said William loudly. I sat.

"What's this? You going to give me breakfast?" I asked.

"I'm going to tell you something that will make your eyes pop, Eddie." He smiled. It wasn't a friendly smile.

I looked at him warily; you always have to look that way when dealing with William.

"Interested in hearing it, Eddie? You should be. It's good news for you. You can go home, back to your flat."

"What do you mean?"

"I mean I've done you a good turn. Like you said, Eddie, it wouldn't look good for the Ginley name if you were found in possession of a corpse and couldn't give a reasonable explanation for it."

"Get to the punch-line," I snapped. So he did.

127

He got to his feet and got to the punch-line; he bellowed it loud and clear.

"I got rid of the body for you!" he shouted. "It cost me two hundred bloody quid, but I got rid of it for you. And do you know why? Because you're my brother. I hate every inch of your crawling little frame, but you're my brother." He sank to the chair. "You're my sodding brother," he subsided.

There wasn't much I could say to follow that. Except to ask where the body was now.

"Where's the body now then?"

"On a boat. Or off a boat. In the Irish Sea."

"You are really Mr Fix-it, aren't you, brother?"

"I'm glad to see you're properly ungrateful," he said.

"Oh! I'm grateful. I really am. Thanks, schmok," I said.

"Get out!" he said. "Get out!"

"I'll send you a proper letter of appreciation, William."

"You're all heart," he said.

"It runs in the family," I reminded him.

Ellen said nothing; she poured herself another cup of tea, and one for William. Another day for the Ginley family it looked. Just another day to get through.

I went out and home.

It was true. My flat was as I'd left it, nothing in it that wasn't mine, and nobody in it to surprise me. I'd never have known there'd been a corpse there if I hadn't been told. So it had been got rid of and I was clear. That didn't help matters. It shouldn't

128

have been there in the first place. Not in my flat. Not anywhere. The guy had given me a beating but I'd liked him. It shouldn't have happened to him, or anyone.

I had a wash, a shave and changed my shirt. I was dog tired. The bed looked inviting. Too bad. I had things to do.

CHAPTER TEN

The British Rail Red Star service is pretty good. You want to send a parcel to a friend? You take it to your local main line station, get it stamped Red Star and it goes off on the next scheduled train to the town where your friend lives; he just picks it up from his local main line station. It helps, of course, to stick your friend's name on, care of the station, then you can be sure it gets to him. The man at the bookshop hadn't done that, he'd marked the package 'Atlantis, c/o Lime Street Station', just like the one I'd got at the hotel. That one had come to me. So had the new one. I went to the Red Star office, signed for it and took it; as simple as that. The fat man didn't know that. He knew someone had taken it, of course. The man at the window of the office was telling him so. The fat man didn't like it. He was bellowing about writing to Head Office. I could see it all: "Dear Mr Manager of British Rail, the Parcels Office at Lime Street Station gave someone else a carton of heroin belonging to me. I wish to complain most strongly…" I should cocoa. With a final, ear-shattering imprecation to the parcels man about his parentage, the fat man waddled furiously off up the platform. He was big as well as fat, and the black, double-breasted coat that flapped around him as he moved looked as though it might be useful for Chipperfield's Circus if they ever lost their tent. He wore a black homburg hat above his purple, fleshy, big-nosed face and fat or not he was fast on his feet. I was not so much tailing him as trotting to keep up with him.

He trundled across the forecourt of the station and got into the driving seat of a Humber Imperial. He was turning on the ignition as I tapped on the window. He looked up and mouthed "What?" at me through the glass. I took my hand out of my trench pocket, holding up the package so he could see it. He rolled down the window.

"You looking for this?" I asked. He looked greedily at the parcel and his big paws came through the window to take it. I stepped back and shoved the package back into my pocket. Big pale eyes came up to meet mine, he bit his lip nervously, but when he spoke he didn't sound nervous. His voice was one I knew, flat, expressionless.

"Police?" he asked.

I shook my head.

"You want money?" he said.

"A name."

"What?"

"Whose," I corrected him. "Yours."

The pale eyes blinked, and he frowned as though struggling to remember his name, I helped him.

"I'm going to yell copper."

"De Fries," he said. "You must be Ginley."

"Ten out of ten, fat man. You want to be careful with your parcels."

"I'll remember," he said.

I walked round the front of the car and got into the passenger seat. "You gave me a gun at the Exchange," I reminded him.

"Did I?" he said without interest.

I pulled out the gun. "You'll notice I still have it," I said.

He shrugged his massive shoulders.

"Nobody's perfect," he said.

I pushed the gun at him. I was getting used to pushing guns at people. I was getting good at it, too. I was getting to realise the obvious – people tend to do things you tell them to when you push guns at them; I hoped I wasn't getting to like doing it.

"Let's go to your place, De Fries."

He started the car. He started to sweat.

He took me to a room on Bedford Street, where the slums met the encroaching newness of the University. He lived on the second floor of what must have been, once, a grand home.

The room was large, high-ceilinged, and had two big windows looking across the street to the slums opposite and the School of Oriental Medicine beyond. There was a table in the middle of the room holding several dirty milk bottles, a packet of tea and a teapot, a bowl of sugar with several dirty spoons in it, a small bunsen burner and a trestle and crucible. There was a wide, low single bed that looked specially strengthened to take De Fries' weight, grey blankets and an equally grey sheet and pillow. There was an old leather armchair, spilling its stuffing onto the floor, and a poster on the wall showing the good life to be had in the Orange Free State. Near a half-open door leading to a bathroom stood some cases with lots of labels stuck on them. I looked at the labels.

"You a travelling man, Mr De Fries?" I asked him. He stood by the bed, tugging at his now damp shirt collar.

"Give me the carton," he said.

I took it out of my pocket and put it on the table. I took out the Smith & Wesson and laid it on top of the package.

"Soon as I have a few answers, De Fries."

He shrugged himself out of his coat and jacket, threw them on the bed and took the bunsen, trestle and crucible from the table to the fireplace. He knelt down and, taking the rubber lead from a gas point set in the fireplace, attached it to the bunsen. He put the trestle over the bunsen and the crucible on the trestle. He stood up, his shirt now wet with perspiration. The pale eyes were begging, the voice remained flat.

"Please give me the carton, Ginley," he said.

"I'll pour it down the can, if I don't get some answers," I threatened him.

"What answers?"

134

"You gave me a package at the hotel, I trailed that package to a bookshop in London. The guy there fingered you. A guy followed me down to London. Name of Straker. Know him?"

He said nothing.

"Nobody knew I was going except my sister-in-law. Name of Ellen. Know her?"

He wasn't saying, so I picked up the package. "I'm flushing this down the toilet." That did it.

"I met her at receptions," he said.

"What receptions?"

"Chamber of Commerce. That sort of thing."

"She's a friend of yours, then?"

"I know her, is all."

"She tell you I was going to London? She ask you to send your hood Straker after me?"

"She didn't tell me you were going anywhere."

"But you knew I was going," I persisted.

"I knew."

"From whom?"

"The others."

"What others?" He looked at me sullenly.

"Flush goes the dope," I said.

"Mrs Blankerscoon."

"Red-haired dame. American?"

"She's no American. She spent a lot of time there, that's all."

"She offered me a phoney job."

"She went to find out from you what you knew."

"What does she want with Alison Wyatt?"

"They don't want anything with her."

"Straker told me he didn't want her, he wanted the money. Now you tell me Blankerscoon doesn't

135

want the girl, so she must want something else. What is it?"

"They want the girl's father. He's in hiding."

"Where would that be?"

"Back home."

"Come on, fat man, where's home?"

"South Africa."

"Why do they want her father?"

"He's a Communist. A troublemaker. If we have the girl he'll come out of hiding."

"Where have they taken her?"

"I don't know."

I walked to the bathroom door.

"Honestly, I don't know," he cried, his face pleading.

"It's not that big a city and yours doesn't sound that big an organisation, De Fries, so why don't you know where she is?"

"They suspect me. I gave you the stuff at the hotel. They think I'm working a double-cross."

"Is she safe?"

"Yes. I told you they want her so they can get her father."

"How do you know she's safe?"

"I just know."

"Her boy friend got killed."

"He was just a black man that got in the way."

Just like that, he said it. Matter of fact. A black man who got in the way.

"People get in my way every day, fat man, what do you suggest I do? Kill them?"

"You don't understand, Ginley. They're obstacles."

"Tell that to Eldridge Cleaver."

"Obstacles to human progress. They don't want what you and I want."

"I don't think you and I want the same thing, fatty. I want a life of my own in my own country. Sounds like Azinge wanted the same thing. I want a lot more besides, and not just for me. They'd be looking for me, too, in your country. I'd be a Communist."

"Azinge wasn't South African. He was a Nigerian."

"Tut, tut. He's no obstacle either, now, is he? Not since you stuck him in my flat."

"You're a fool, Ginley. What do you hope to gain from this? Who's behind you? Why did you turn up at the hotel? What are you trying to do?"

"You wouldn't understand, De Fries. You wouldn't begin to understand. You see, I subscribe to a different view of what we're here for. I read in a book once that if someone cries in the night, you go and see what's wrong with them. I'm trying to see that nobody needs to cry alone."

"A stupid idealist, Ginley, a stupid idealist."

"I told you that you wouldn't understand. I'm no idealist, De Fries, I just believe man is capable of most anything, once he's organised. And one of the things he's capable of, when the crap hits the fan as it surely will one day in your country, is seeing that there is no place for you and yours to run to. When the whistle blows on your lot, De Fries, there will be nowhere for you to go. You're a big bundle of nothing."

I had a lot more to say but didn't get round to

saying it. The door bell rang and there was a race for the window in which De Fries beat me by a short head. We stared down at the street. We couldn't see who was at the front door but we could see the big, black Daimler parked behind De Fries' Humber. De Fries turned to me, babbling.

"They'll kill me, Ginley! They'll kill me! If they even smell you've been here I've had it."

"Where's the way out?"

"There's no way out except by the front door. They'll kill me! I know it."

"Shut up !" I barked at him. I went to the table and grabbed the gun.

"I'll be in the bathroom, De Fries; I've got your package and I've got the gun. If you tell them I'm here you don't get the junk but I get you."

I hoped it was enough. He scuttled out of the room, I stepped into the bathroom. The door was one of those half-wood, half-glass affairs. The glass was frosted.

The hinges were so rotten that the door wouldn't close. There was a gap of a couple of inches or so between the edge of the door and the jamb. I looked around. The bath was pitted with rust and stained with green splotches. There was a handbasin with a shelf above it holding De Fries' shaving materials and a small mirror. Next to the basin was the toilet and above that a small window. There was no way out and nowhere to hide. I wished I hadn't been so declamatory with De Fries. I wished I was at home. I wished I had left well alone in the first place. I wished my shirt didn't cling damply to me. It was no use wishing.

138

I heard De Fries come back into the room, saying:

"Where did you get it?"

Then came the voice of the red-haired dame, Blankerscoon.

"Easier than you think, Jacob. You could have been a lot more open about it to us, you know. Here. What do you do with it?"

I peered through the door-gap to see De Fries light the bunsen burner. He poured a white powder from a small cellophane bag into the crucible. A few moments later he picked up the crucible and disappeared from sight. There was the sound of objects being moved around the table and when I looked again I could see De Fries sitting on the edge of the bed with the rubber hose from the gas point wound round his bare arm and held taut by his teeth. His fist was tight round a black rubber ball and with his left hand he was about to give himself an injection. He squeezed the hypodermic into the air to see that it was working, then plunged it into his arm. Very professionally. I closed my eyes and as I did so I heard a man's voice, in a tight South African accent, say:

"Couldn't he do it in the bathroom?"

I held my breath and my hand tightened on the Smith & Wesson in my pocket.

"For God's sake, don't look if you can't stand it," Mrs Blankerscoon said. Then, "Finished, Jacob?"

"What now?" said the South African voice,

"Take the cases downstairs," she said.

I heard him by the bathroom door, lugging the cases.

139

"Anything else?" he asked.

"Just take the cases, Clifford, and wait for me in the car."

I heard the door open and the man going out.

"What's it like Jacob?" she said.

"It helps," said De Fries, "It just helps. It used to be wonderful. It used to be like–" He stopped. "You'd laugh at me."

"I won't, I promise," she said.

"It used to be like I was dancing. Dancing on fields of eggs. And not breaking them because I was so light. So very light."

"That's a lovely thought, Jacob," she said.

"Now it just helps," he said. "I go cold, then I sweat and the pain starts. It helps. It stops all that."

There was a sound on the stairs and I heard the door opening.

"I told you to stay in the car," Mrs Blankerscoon spat.

"I thought you might need help," said Clifford.

"Here? With him? He's finished."

"What time do we have?"

"We leave the house at five. We want to be on board two hours before, at least."

"What about him?"

"Him?" She started to laugh. "He's going home too, isn't he?"

"What's going on?" a drowsy De Fries said. I looked through the door. De Fries was lying back on the bed. I couldn't see the others.

"We were just talking about the arrangements for going home, Jacob," said Mrs Blankerscoon, "Clifford and I are going to pack now. We've taken your things. You clean yourself up and we'll come back for you."

"We really going home?" De Fries said, almost in a whisper. I had to strain hard to hear.

"We're really going home, Jacob."

"It's going to take a lot to get him out of here," said Clifford.

"Shut up!" she snapped. "Come on!"

I heard the door close and feet on the stairs. I waited. Below, I heard the sound of a door bang. I opened the bathroom door and crossed to the window. The Daimler was pulling out from behind the Humber. It roared off up the street. I turned to look at De Fries. He lay awkwardly back on the bed, his feet on the floor. His eyes were closed and tears streaked his cheeks.

"Okay, De Fries, the lady said she was leaving at five and had to be on board two hours before. Leaving from where? On board what? Five p.m. or a.m.?"

He didn't reply. I went across and shook him. He took a lot of shaking with his massive bulk – all I managed to do was to roll a bit of his fat about.

"Come on, De Fries, snap it up!"

He didn't move. I picked up his right arm. It was limp, and when I let go of it, it fell and the knuckles of his hand hit the floor with a clunk. From his palm, the rubber ball rolled across the floor. He didn't wake up. He didn't make a sound. He didn't need me, he didn't need Christiaan Barnard, he didn't need anyone. I went into the bathroom, put my head over the toilet and puked up the tea I'd had at William and Ellen's that morn-

141

ing. I've been present at death in our family. That's one thing. You never get used to it. I'd never been present at a murder before. That was something else. You get even less used to that.

I went back into the room. I found the syringe, the rubber hose and the ball and loaded them into my handkerchief. I folded it and put it carefully into the pocket of my trench. I didn't look at De Fries again. I got the hell out of there.

I wandered about for a bit, trying, vainly, to clear my mind of what I had seen. There was traffic on the roads, people on the pavements. None of them knew what I knew. They were going about their normal business. Only I knew there was a murdered man in a room in Bedford Street. Only I, and the woman who murdered him. And Clifford, who was probably out looking for a box big enough to ship him home in. To ship home the poor fat slob they'd left to do his dying in a crummy room in a slum; alone. I read somewhere that one of the dangers of addiction is that, besides eventually killing the addict, it can kill him a lot sooner if he shoots up with stuff that's too impure. Most junk is mixed with other things, of course, that render it impure. That's how the rats who sell it can make it go round further and reap a bigger profit. Also, if junk is absolutely pure, it can finish you off in seconds flat. It's too powerful for the system. That's what I figured had happened to De Fries. There's no way you can win with junk.

I had a crazy impulse to stop someone on the street and tell them all of this, but I didn't. I found a telephone box, 'phoned the *Echo*, and told them.

142

I told them I'd seen a guy murdered by a lady giving him a dose of pure heroin. I told them that's what I guessed, anyway, but that whatever she'd given him was enough to do for a dinosaur. I told them where they could find the body. I told them to be quick because there would be an attempt made to ship the body out of the country. I told them that all concerned were South African diplomats. They heard all this and sounded excited. I rang off without saying who I was. Then I went into town.

It was twelve-fifty and people were spilling out of the Liver building for lunch as I pushed my way past them. Inside, I looked at the notice board, found what I wanted and got into the lift. I got out on the fifth floor and followed the arrows around until I found the place I wanted. The pebbled glass double doors read 'Botha Ltd. General Office and Enquiries. Please enter.' I entered.

The office was small and cramped. Green metal filing cabinets crowded into a small desk in the centre of the room. Behind it sat a girl exercising her social conscience, reading *Nova*. There was a name block on the desk, it read 'Miss Joan Bamford'. To the left of the desk between the filing cabinets was the door to an inner office. The legend on the door read 'Managing Director'. I coughed.

From behind the magazine a piping cockney voice said, "We're closing for lunch. Come back at two o'clock."

"Board of Trade. We have powers of search."

The magazine was lowered and a blonde, attractive girl looked at me and then at the folded

143

dole card. I put the card away. She looked me over slowly, like a fellow undresses a girl with his eyes.

"You don't look like the Board of Trade." I changed my mind, the voice was more of a squeak than a pipe.

"We're changing the image," I said. "Hey!"

"What?"

"Don't move," I warned. "You've got something on your eye." I walked across to the desk and leant across it. She reached a hand to her face.

"Wrong eye. Don't touch it. Now, close them."

She did as she was bid. I leant in further and kissed her. It was nice. I don't know why I did it except that I probably figured that it was about time something nice happened to me. She opened her eyes and looked at me.

"I was telling a lie," I said.

"Out goes old style, fuddy-duddy, Board of Trade," she said.

"Something like that."

"We've only just met."

"Give it time," I told her.

"I don't think I fancy you."

"Work on it."

She stood up. I leaned off the desk and stood up too. She was about five foot eleven. She looked down at my five seven.

"You're too small," she said.

"The Seven Dwarfs got Snow White," I reminded her.

"That's because they crowded her," she said.

"You could go down on your knees for me."

"On this floor?" The squeak was outraged.

144

"I could put a cushion down," I offered.

"I couldn't."

"Why not?"

"I stoop to conquer, I don't kneel."

Educated, too.

"Know anyone called Mrs Blankerscoon?"

"You kidding?" she asked. "She's never off the bloody 'phone."

"She expected here?"

"No, she's leaving the country."

"When?"

"Tomorrow morning."

"How?" I asked.

"Boat. Huskisson Dock."

"Do you have an address for her?" I asked.

"49, Faulkner Square," she said. "Why?"

"Nothing. Listen, when we were out together I'd walk behind you."

She shook her head. "I like to hold hands," she said.

"So?"

"It would look like I was taking you for a walk."

"Defy convention."

"I'm basically conservative."

"Switch sides."

"I'd rather fight than switch."

"In that case our relationship is doomed," I said. "Mind if I use the 'phone?"

"Be my guest," she said.

I called Tommy at the club and asked if I could see him. He told me to tell him for what over the telephone, but I told him I couldn't because the line might be tapped. When he asked who'd tap

145

his line, I told him the Copacabana and he was still trying to figure it out when I rang off.

I also called the Mossley Hill number and made an arrangement to meet at the club. I put down the 'phone.

"You'd rather fight than switch?"

"Always," said Miss Bamford.

"What weight do you fight at?"

"Heavy," she said.

"What's a nice London heavyweight doing here?"

"The old story," she said. "I was in a dance troupe when the manager ran off with the money and I was stranded. So I took this job here. Temporarily like. Dancing's my career."

"You got stranded in *this* town?"

"Ridiculous, isn't it," she said.

I walked to the door. I turned. "I've got a long reach," I said.

"No good in a clinch," she said, and grinned.

"Keep your guard up, don't lead with your chin, and keep poking out those lefts."

"What for?" she asked.

"You could get a crack at the title," I said, and left. There are certain people who don't deserve secretaries like her, I thought as I walked to the lift.

The white Lotus Europa was outside the Broadway when I got there. Ellen was inside watching the show. Tommy puts on a show, two afternoons a week, for the old age pensioners. They get tea and buns in the interval; I suppose it helps to pass the time away for them. Ellen sat at a table by the door. I sat down opposite her. She didn't look at me, she kept her eyes on the act on stage: a magician.

"How apt," I said.

"What do you mean?" she asked.

"The magician. He's showing his tricks and you play tricks."

"I don't get you."

"Forget it."

"Where were you ringing from?"

"William's office. I had a very instructive time in his office. It's a pity he wasn't there."

"Why don't we go away together, Eddie?"

"You serious?"

"Why shouldn't I be?"

"Where would we go?"

"Anywhere. London."

"What would we do there?"

"You could get a job."

"Ex-comic. Unskilled. And you?"

"You could do anything. You've got a degree."

"I've got a lot of degrees, they're all on a thermometer. I said what about you?"

"It wouldn't matter what I did. I've got some money."

"We're not married."

She turned to look at me for the first time since I came into the club.

"Do we have to be?" she whispered.

"I'm old-fashioned," I told her.

"Defy convention."

I grinned, "I just said that to somebody else."

"We could simply run away together."

147

"The last time a guy ran off with his sister-in-law, England went Protestant."

The magician produced a dove from his hat, the audience clapped, the curtains closed and Sammy came on stage.

"Okay, lads and lasses," Sammy said. "Take your hands off each others ha'pennies. Tea and buns are served at the bar. Bingo in fifteen minutes."

The lights went up; the O.A.P.s surged past us for the refreshments.

"William ships stuff to Africa," she said,

"Yeah. Gardening tools to Mozambique."

"To Rhodesia. Parts for cars. Chemicals. Anything they want. It makes him a lot of money."

"You too, love, you too. Tell me something new."

"Have I told you lately that I love you?"

"Now you're beginning to hurt, Ellen, hurt my intelligence. You shouldn't do that, kid, it doesn't become you. Let's talk about something else."

"Like what?"

"Like why we're here. A girl called Alison Wyatt was snatched. That night I turned up at your house with the gun, my birthday, remember? I'd got sicked into it. I don't know why." I paused, giving her time to let everything sink in.

"The spade, Azinge, you found dead in my flat – he was her boyfriend-bodyguard. She's wanted back in South Africa to flush her old man out of the bush. They're shipping her out. Guess who's boxing her up?"

She essayed a grin, it didn't quite take.

"Is this the old style, live-for-today Fast Eddie Ginley I'm listening to?"

"No, baby, it's the new-style, weary, wary, what's-all-this-crap-about-running-away-together, slow Eddie Ginley you're hearing."

"We could have good times together, Eddie," she said softly.

"Wrong tense, kid. We could have *had* good times together. You're married, I keep telling you. You've been married a year now. It should have sunk in."

"It takes two to make a marriage, Eddie."

"It takes two to keep one as well – why not give it a try?"

"A marriage that's no good?" she said bitterly, "a husband who's up to his neck in no good?"

"And going with me would be good?"

"It could be Eddie, it could be." She put her hand on mine. I shook it off and went to seek out Tommy.

In the back bar all was quiet at this time of day. I suppose the back bar of the Broadway is what you might call 'swish provincial' – leatherette seating round the walls, low tables, easy chairs. Behind the bar, towelling a few glasses, was Joey Oliver. Joey, besides being barman, is in charge of the club when Tommy's not there. He's tall and stout is Joey, mild-mannered, too. You would never think he was an ex-Desert Rat. Unless you buy him a drink and ask him about Tobruk then he'll drag out his wallet and show the cutting from a war-time *Echo* that his mam kept for him, telling of his escape from an Italian P.O.W. camp and his

149

'mentioned-in-despatches'. He's a tough customer is Joey. He fought Rommel. Rommel lost.

"Tommy's in the office, Eddie," said Joey.

"Do us a favour, Joey?" I asked.

"Anything."

"Send out for a paper."

"I'll go myself. I'm doing sod all here."

"Ta."

I knocked on the office door and went in. Tommy was hanging up another picture.

"Hello, Eddie, what do you think of this?" He stepped back from the wall and I looked at the new photograph. It was Tommy, of course, with his arm round someone I didn't recognise – a woman in 1930s dress by the look of it. "Who is it?" I asked him.

"Read it."

I did. "To a dish from a Gish. Love to Tommy from Lillian."

"Lillian Gish," he said.

"Go on."

"No kidding, it's Lillian Gish."

"It's terrific."

"I thought you'd like it," he said. "She's always been a favourite of mine. Still going, she is."

"You don't say?"

"Yeah." He grinned and settled himself comfortably behind his desk. "What's the favour, lad?"

"A couple."

"What's the first?"

"49, Faulkner Square."

"Well?"

150

"I want to know about it."

"Housebreaking, Eddie?"

I shook my head.

"Second favour?"

"When I know about the house."

"A 'phone call."

"I'll be out front."

I went back into the club. Ellen was sitting where I had left her. Joey stood behind her chair. On stage the 'Broadway Trio', organ, bass guitar and drums, escapees from the Saturated Seven, were running through a selection of old favourites. As I took the paper from Joey and sat down, the audience were singing softly: "For it was Mary, Mary, plain as any name could be." Joey went out.

I looked at her. "I used to wonder why a great-looking chick used to hang around a guy like me. That's why I treated you so badly, I guess, I couldn't figure the angles."

"Couldn't you?"

"No."

"Maybe there weren't any angles, Eddie. Maybe I hung around you, as you put it, because I wanted to." She paused. "Wanted you." She smiled sadly; it was a private smile to herself.

I unfolded the paper; it had made the headlines.

DIPLOMAT MURDERED?
Mystery 'phone call to *Echo*.

The story pretty much recounted my 'phone call and the story of a reporter finding the body and telling the police. It didn't say what the police were doing, but it never does. I held the paper up

151

for Ellen to see. She read it and her face began to crumple, so I fished for my handkerchief and held it across.

"I'm not going to cry," she said in a choked voice. Nevertheless, she took the handkerchief.

"I didn't think you would," I said as she dabbed at her face. "Name of De Fries. Did you know?"

"Did I know *him*?" she asked.

"Did you know they murdered him?"

Her head bowed. "I saw him die, Ellen," I went on. "I saw a lady, ever so much a lady, pump that billiard ball so full of junk that he rolled into the pocket and stayed there."

Well, it was near enough to the truth to make the point.

"Junk?" she said.

"It wasn't Kelloggs. That same lady also had the guy killed in my flat. She also snatched Alison Wyatt. She employed De Fries. De Fries knew you. William's in business with them. He's married to you. I'm not telling you anything new, I just want to know where you fit in?"

"For God's sake, that's all it is, business. I only saw them at trade receptions. I'll take you along sometime," she snapped.

I grinned at her; I didn't feel much like grinning.

"Isn't it wonderful?" I said. "They hold trade receptions for sanctions busters, kidnappers and murderers. Tory freedom really works."

"You could get hurt, Eddie."

"Is that why you want us to go away? Because I could get hurt?"

152

"And because of me," she said softly.

"Speak up, baby," I said, "the music's very loud."

"You heard," she said.

I'd heard all right.

"I'm thirty-one years old. I've got ten more instalments to pay before I own my hi-fi, and I want to be around to finish paying them. I'm unemployed, I'm looking for a job, it's exciting. You've got no offer to match that. Besides, I've got a lot of speed and I want to use it."

The audience clapped as the trio finished. Ellen looked across to me.

"Do you think they had a lot of speed?" she asked, nodding at the O.A.P.s.

"Probably. But it's a tough life. There's a whole world of Williams out there," I said.

"What do they do then?" she asked.

"Nothing much. Wait. And play bingo. It's all that a lot of them have got."

The trio struck up again and the audience cooed softly into "Oh How We Danced on the Night We Were Wed". I looked around. At the next table an old couple were holding hands and looking at each other as they sang, trying to remember the words, perhaps trying to conjure up the feelings they had had on the night *they* were wed.

Tea, buns and bingo. There's got to be something better than this for them, I thought. For all of us. That's the way to think. That's what to work for.

"What do we do now?" she said.

"Where do you stand, kid?"

"Haven't I made it clear? Is that why you called me out here? To tell you again and again? To reassure you?"

"I don't mean that."

"Then I don't know what you mean."

"Shall I make it clear to you, Ellen? Tell *you* again and again? It won't reassure you. It's just the old story, baby. Don't act dumb. It's too late."

"Is that all?"

"No. I want you to give a message to Mrs Blankerscoon. Tell her the comic's taken a back seat. Tell her the private investigator's back in business. She'll understand."

She looked down at my handkerchief in her palm. She held it out to me.

"I gave you these for your birthday," she said.

"That was several birthdays ago." I took the handkerchief.

"They're initialled," she said.

"I noticed."

"E for Eddie."

"E for enough, which is what I've had."

We got up and went out to the foyer. We stood at the door looking out at a late, grey afternoon. Tommy called me from the back door. I went in.

"That address, Eddie."

"Yeah?"

"Nothing known. It's a rented house near one of the Consulates. Portuguese. The fellow I spoke to reckons some foreigners live in the place, but he doesn't know if they're Portuguese. They run a late model Daimler. They keep it at the back."

"Thanks, Tommy."

154

"None of the lads have ever knocked the place over. 'Course now I've put a whisper out about it there'll probably be a queue there tonight."

"I hope not."

"What was the second favour?"

"A car and a driver."

"That address?"

"Yeah."

"To pipe or rumble?"

I shrugged, "It could be rough."

"Joey. He's muscle," said Tommy. "You know his war record."

"I know it. There are some people in that house I want to talk to."

"You want in, or them out?"

"Them out. I don't care how. But they're definitely not going to come if I ask nicely."

He paused a moment to think, then he smiled.

"Got a lighter?" he asked.

"A Zippo."

"What time do you want Joey?"

"Tomorrow morning. Early."

"How early is 'early'?"

"About half-four."

"Will do, Eddie."

"Can you keep him awake?"

Tommy smirked. "For you, Eddie? He'll wear his tin hat."

I smirked back. "You shoot good pool, Tommy."

"Listen," he said.

"I'm listening."

"Listen," he started to go red.

"I'm listening."

"Come and see us when…" he tailed off.

"See you when?"

"When… when you and Joey do whatever… Come and see us, will you?" Tommy didn't know where to look. He never does when he gets embarrassed.

"Sure."

He held out his hand, "You're a good lad, Eddie. Take care," he mumbled.

I shook his hand. I went out to the foyer. No Ellen.

I walked into the car park. The Lotus had gone. I looked at my watch. It was six o'clock. I set off to walk back into town. It's seven miles from the club to the city.

I took it slowly. I had a lot of time to kill.

Faulkner Square is a beautiful piece of Georgian planning. A piece of history in a city that's fast burying any antiquity it still has. Four lines of elegant houses facing on to railed-in overgrown grass and unkempt bushes. Ranks of sad-looking trees line the pavements. Even the peeling stucco of the exteriors can't detract from the symmetry of the architecture. Even the knowledge that inside those edifices that are not consulates live families in slum conditions cannot distract you from the sense of the past you get when you stand in the square. It bloody well should, though, I thought, as I tried to stamp warmth into my body that wintry morning.

I stood by the railings, under a tree next to the telephone box, on the pavement opposite number

156

49. It was a corner house, next but one to the Portuguese Consulate. The Portuguese have a lot to answer for around the world, one way and another, I told myself. I just hoped the Consulate and 49 didn't have a connecting passage of any sort.

A Cortina turned slowly into the Square on the opposite side to where I was. I took out a fag and started to light it as I ambled off up the pavement like a home-coming reveller on the off-chance it was a prowl car – in plain clothes as it were. But it was Joey. He pulled over to the kerb and I got in.

"It's bloody cold, Eddie, isn't it?" Joey said, He looked even bigger than he usually does as he sat there in his donkey jacket. He'd put the wind up me, would Joey, never mind Rommel. He wasn't wearing his tin hat, though, only a flat green cheese-cutter.

"Where's the stuff?"

"On the dash," he said.

I took out a brown paper carrier bag like the ones they give you in off-licences to take your ale home. I looked inside.

"Okay," I said.

"When do we go?"

"After we've had a ciggy." I lit a new one from my stub and offered him the packet. It was very peaceful as we sat there smoking.

"What was it like fighting Rommel, Joey?" I asked him.

"Personally, Eddie, I never saw the bugger. I saw James Mason being Rommel in a film once. Couldn't stand it. All them good Germans. You know when toddlers today grow up they'll wonder what all the fuss was about in the last war – just one mad sod trying to take over the world and all his country against him. All the krauts against him, but not letting on, you know. All honourable men, really," he sighed, "I've never been since."

"You've missed a lot of good movies."

"I mean I've never been to war films since," he corrected me. "Give me musicals every time. Or Westerns for that matter. I'm not particular."

"I know how you feel." I rolled down the window and threw the cigarette out. Joey nodded to the house.

"Wouldn't going in be simpler?"

"I don't know exactly how many there are in there."

"Why don't we wait till they come out?"

"Because I want them out on my terms."

"There aren't any lights. What if they're out already?"

"Then we'll be up to our necks in the brown and sticky." Joe stubbed his fag into the dash ash tray.

"Ready, lad," he said in his best army manner, and rubbed his hands expectantly.

"Okay, Joey. I've piped the back of the house. There's an alley blocked off at one end. They can only move out this end. The alley comes out into the street at the side of the house." I pointed.

"Gotcha," he said.

"When I give you the wire I want you to stick the car across the end of the alley."

"Right."

158

"Right."

I picked up the carrier and got out of the car. I walked across to the telephone box, went in and plonked the carrier on the floor. The box had been vandalised but it was still possible to get the emergency services. I'd made sure of that. I dialled 999 and asked for Fire. I was put through to the calm voice of a girl saying, "This is the Fire Service."

I answered her by bellowing into the 'phone, "There's a fire! A fire at 49, that's four, nine, Faulkner Square. Faulkner Square. Got that?"

The girl said, "Take it easy, sir."

"But there's a fire!" I shrieked into the receiver. "It's not my house. I was just passing and I saw it. 49, Faulkner Square. Hurry up!" I slammed down the telephone, picked up the bag and walked out of the box across the road.

I opened the carrier, took out a lemonade bottle filled with a colourless liquid and stuffed with a long rag that hung out from the top of the bottle. I took out my Zippo and walked up the path of the house. I lit the rag and without waiting to see if the flame took I bashed the bottle through the window of 49.

I ran back across the street to the car and waited. In the distance could be heard the sound of clanging bells coming nearer. I looked at the house. A light had come on upstairs but nothing else was happening. I looked at Joey. He shrugged as if to say "Well, we tried." I looked back at the house. Nothing.

Three fire engines screamed up the street, bells going like all get out. Lights started to dot the houses around the square. The leading engine squealed to a stop and a fireman leapt down. He looked at 49 and went back to the cab of the fire engine. The driver handed down a 'phone to him and he started to speak into it. The 'phone was amplified and from the car we could clearly hear the fireman say, "Arrived 49 Faulkner Square. False alarm. Repeat, False alarm."

Then the window blew out and great tongues of flame shot across to the pavement and up the walls of the house.

"Okay Joey," I said, and ran across the street to the house. The front door opened and Clifford appeared in chauffeur's uniform. He looked wildly at the scene that met his eyes, shouted "Jesus Christ!" and slammed the door shut again. Taking him to be the demented owner, two firemen started to hack at the door with axes.

I ran along the side of the house to reach the alley. As I turned into it Clifford was jumping into the driving seat of the big, black Daimler I had seen outside De Fries' pad. He'd moved fast, had Clifford, to get from the front door to the car before me, but then I had a feeling that he was a spring-bok in a chauffeur's suit. The car was facing me, blocking the alley, about twenty-five yards away. The engine was running as Clifford leapt in and he seemed to close the door and crash the car into gear at the same time.

The Daimler barrelled up the alley towards me; I was too far up the alley to go back and I certainly couldn't go forward over the car. To the left of me was the door to someone's back yard. Praying that it wasn't locked, I threw myself at it. As I hit the wood it gave and I fell inwards, hitting a bin which overturned, taking me with it.

I heard a great crunching sound and hoped it wasn't my head, hitting concrete. It wasn't. The sky hadn't fallen.

I got up smelling of refuse, and with my arm aching, but I hadn't taken the count. I was shaken, but since I could hear Clifford shouting some very un-Dutch Reformed Church imprecations I reckoned I was okay.

Outside, the Daimler had come to a dead stop at the top of the alley. It had come to a dead stop because it had hit the side of the alley in braking to avoid hitting Joey's Cortina which he had driven across the exit to the street. Neither Joey nor Clifford had left their driving seats. Neither was taking a chance.

I went round the left, undamaged, side of the Daimler and pulled open the passenger door. Joey rolled down the window of the Cortina.

"Okay, Eddie?" Joey shouted.

"Sure thing. Move your heap, Joey, and stick with us."

I got into the back of the Daimler, pulled down the rumble seat, sat and surveyed the scene. On the back seat of that cavernous vehicle sat two thirds of the Ginley family and the red-haired dame, Mrs Blankerscoon. I turned to the front, Alison Wyatt was in the passenger seat next to Clifford. There was one of those glass partition affairs to separate the paid help from the gentry. It was wound half down so that, presumably, conversation could

161

flow between the five gadabouts. I took out the Smith & Wesson and rested it on Clifford's starched white collar.

"There will be a lot of firemen and policemen here soon, Cliff, so get going."

"We haven't got much time if we are to make the boat," Clifford said, but not to me.

"You've got nearly two hours – *if* you make it, Clifford – so unless you want a lead earring, get moving," I said.

"Do as he says, Clifford," said Mrs Blankerscoon.

Clifford moved the car. He swung it right, onto the street, away from the conflagration at the front of the house. I looked through the darkened window at the back of the car; Joey was following us.

William and Ellen did not seem elated at my sudden appearance. William sat looking fiercely at me, clutching a black leather briefcase to himself, like a frontier mother protecting her baby when the Indians appear. Ellen, sullen, looked at the floor. To give her her due, Mrs Blankerscoon, if not quite taking me in her stride, at least made an attempt at some composure.

I looked at William.

"What's in the briefcase, brother? Money? Passports? Toothbrush and paste? I apologise for giving you-all no time to pack."

"We've got to get to the boat," Clifford reminded them.

"Your needle's stuck," I told him.

"Don't panic, Clifford, this won't take long," said the Blankerscoon woman.

I smiled at her.

"By the way," I said, "I've been meaning to ask you. Why the boat? What happened to 'planes? They just a passing fad? I thought there was a South African airline, or do even they quibble at kidnappers?"

"No-one hi-jacks boats," said Clifford in what may have attempted to be a joke.

"What do you want, Ginley?" said Mrs Blankerscoon.

"Alison."

"You're very persistent," she said.

"That's us gumshoes' stock in trade, lady," I quipped. "You'll be familiar with the term by the way?"

"Gumshoe? My time in America wasn't entirely wasted," she said.

"That where you copped for the phoney accent? Where abouts in America?"

"Michigan. Ann Arbor," and she smiled as she said it,

"Their standards must really be low. I was at the University of Hull. We must swap old academic chat some time when you feel up to it," I said.

The smile froze.

"You're a lunatic, Ginley," she snapped.

"Yeah, but I'm covered lady. I got a psychiatric record. What about you?"

"Have I got a psychiatric record?"

"You should have. You murdered De Fries. I was there. You blew up that balloon till he burst. That puts you one step ahead of the men in the white coats."

We were rolling downhill now into the city. Dawn had broken and it looked like it might be a nice day. I hoped I'd be able to get out and about and enjoy it.

William and Ellen still weren't talking. The red-haired phoney was.

"De Fries was cracking up. He gave you the package with the gun. We didn't want the girl killed. That was wrong," she said.

"And killing him was right?"

"He had to go," she said, like she was saying, "it's nine o'clock," or "it's raining."

"He may have given me the gun, lady, but as far as he knew it was on the level. He didn't know I wasn't the one who'd been hired to snatch the girl. That was a guy called Straker. So someone put him up to getting me to the hotel and giving me the rod. And that someone must have given it to him to give to me. Someone on your side has been queering your pitch, missus, why don't you kill them?"

She got even more refrigerated around the chops.

Clifford turned the car out of Bold Street into Church Street and pointed it in the direction of the Pier Head. We must have been doing a steady thirty-five; Joey was chugging along behind.

"You haven't answered," I told her. "Someone's been trying to break up your game by using me and you don't seem to know who."

She opened her mouth to a slit and, "I don't care," slid out.

"You don't care?"

The slit became a crack. "I don't care, Ginley. It's

164

none of your business. Somehow you got into this, but you're getting out now. I'm calling the police."

I looked at William and Ellen; Ellen shot Blankerscoon a terrified glance at the mention of police.

"None of my business?" I said.

"You're not deaf," snapped William.

"None of my business," I repeated. "Two guys get seen off, you try to head me off with the offer of a phoney job, your Scotch broth Straker tries to knock me off for the money, my brother tries to buy me off with a so-called birthday present, his missus tries to take me off to a new life in London, and it's none of my business and you're calling the police. That's what's known as *chutzpa*. You know what that is? That's when a guy murders his mum and dad then begs mercy from the court because he's an orphan. That's what you got lots of, lady."

"I don't think so, Ginley. I think I'm sitting pretty. I'm an accredited commercial attaché representing a country friendly to Britain. I am being assaulted in my own car in the presence of two friends and an employee who will bear witness to that fact to the police. I am attempting to board a boat with those friends and that employee to return home. We are escorting a young South African girl of our acquaintance who also wishes to return home. What's your story?"

"I was there when Mrs Blankerscoon, red-head Caucasian, and her employee killed Jacob De Fries. That's my story."

"And you didn't immediately report the crime to the proper authorities. Tch! Tch! Ginley, that makes you an accessory after the fact."

The car turned onto the Pier Head and drew to a stop at the kerb opposite the bus terminus and landing stage. There were one or two buses parked, waiting for the first passengers of the day. The drivers and conductors lounged against the front of one of the buses, smoking, waiting for the action. They could have had some of mine had they asked.

I turned to the front and looked at the back of Alison's head. She had been silent all through the drive. Now it was her turn.

"Okay, kid, we're getting out," I said to her.

She said nothing. I looked back. Blankerscoon was smiling, Ellen and William were staring at me, watchfully.

I tightened my grip on the .38.

"I can't hear you," I said to Alison.

She didn't turn round to look at me. She just sat there and said quietly, "I'm going home, Eddie."

I tried not to show the shock.

"I think my ears are on the blink, Fats," I almost whispered to her.

"I'm going home," she said again, tonelessly.

"With this lot?" I couldn't take it in.

"I live there, too," she said.

"What are you going to do, baby? You think they're going to let you join your father in the bush?"

"They've caught him," she said.

"So they've caught him. We've caught her," I pointed the gun back at Blankerscoon.

"What do you reckon on, Eddie? To swap her

for my father? I thought you were intelligent. Wise up. The big league's in Johannesburg."

"What are you trying to say, kid? I want to understand."

"What happens if we turn her in here? The Consulate or the Embassy would have her sprung in seconds flat with apologies from the British Government all round. The fight isn't here, Eddie."

"You're forgetting something, aren't you? Someone. Danny Azinge. Your pal. What about him?"

"Danny knew the risks," she whispered, "You must see that, Eddie. It's all right marching and banning cricket tours – we need that – but there's a fight going on too. You don't hear about that here, except when someone like Danny dies in it. Blankerscoon will get hers, Eddie, one day. We'll fix that. But at home. Our way."

"Tell Danny that, love, if you can. He'll really appreciate it," I said, even though I thought her argument right. She started to cry quietly.

I looked at the three on the back seat. Mrs Blankerscoon oozed smug self-assurance.

"You've no shots left to call, Eddie," she said.

"So?"

"It's a pity for you. You know, you have many qualities I admire."

"Flattery will get you a slap in the mouth from the roscoe, lady," I threatened and brought the gun up to add weight to the threat.

"You're stubborn. I like that," she said. "You're loyal, I like that, too."

167

"No kidding."

"There could be a future for you." She turned on an encouraging smile.

"Like where?"

"Where do you think?"

"What kind of a future?"

"Name it."

"Lady, you haven't got it to give."

"Money? Cars? A steady job? Nice house?" she offered.

"You left out women," I told her.

She looked from me to Ellen.

"What about *the* woman?"

I looked at William to see how he took the offer of his wife to me.

"It's a good offer," he said. So much for love. "Is that your alternative?" I said to her.

William spoke again. "It's not an alternative, Eddie, there's nothing else. A dead addict? Anonymous 'phone calls to the paper? Is that all you've got? You're unemployed, Eddie. Where's your pull?"

"That's how it looks, brother," I said.

He laughed. "An ex-comic," he chortled.

"A gone Ginley," I agreed.

"Precisely," he said.

"If I was to tell my story I'd need backing up."

"Absolutely. And who would do that?"

I looked at Ellen.

"I need help, kid," I said to her.

"P for plenty," she said, "which is what you're not going to get." She must have been rehearsing.

"That's funny," I said, "because seeing as you

got me into this, I'd have thought the least you could do was to get me out of it."

Blankerscoon turned furiously on her. "So it was you!" she shouted.

"I was scared!" Ellen cried. "I didn't know what you were going to do to the girl. I thought you would call it off if something went wrong with the arrangements."

"You stupid little bitch!" Blankerscoon spat out.

Ellen appealed to me. "Doing business with William was one thing, but when they started to talk about getting the girl, it was something else! Making money was all right, killing was different! And I didn't know they weren't going to kill her! They kept talking about 'getting her'. It sounded like killing to me."

She put her hands up to her face and sank back in the seat.

"So I was the grit in the wheels, eh, kid? You make money and I take the count. I get trampled on while you make the world safe for capitalism? Is that it?"

"How did you know it was me?" she mumbled from behind her hands.

"I didn't. I guessed. I just thumbed through the dog-eared pages of my mind and came up with the name Ellen. The cool way you acted the night I turned up at your house with the gun. Remember? 'Even you're too old for a toy one, Eddie,' you said. Remember? That was *scared*? I can see you thinking, 'I'll get old Eddie into this. This is just up his alley. He's off his head; with a bit of luck, he'll be off running, with them after him, before he knows what's what.' Thanks a million, sister-in-law."

"It wasn't like that, Eddie," she mumbled. "I didn't like fooling you."

"Really?" I sneered. "I loved it. I thought it was a real yock. As funny as a hole in a lifeboat."

"What's it to be, Eddie?" said Blankerscoon.

"What if I get out of the car, go home and leave you to it?"

"To what, Eddie?" she said. "You know where we put Azinge's body?"

"In my flat."

"That's right. So how can you go home? You'll have to take our offer. I'd like it if you would." She looked at me solicitously.

"Missus, here's something for you to treasure in your old age, if you get that far. Never trust a Ginley. Tell her, brother?" I looked at William.

She shot him a vicious look.

"What the hell is this?"

"Tell her, William. Tell her how you swept up the cadaver."

I got out of the Daimler and Joey got out of the Cortina and came up to me. I walked round the front and tapped on Clifford's window. And they let me, that was what was surprising. I guess it was because they were bickering away in the back, and Clifford, being a true Wehrmacht type, was waiting to follow orders. And he didn't get any. He didn't start the heap up and get the hell out of there, either.

I tapped with the gun on the window. Clifford rolled it down. I leaned across him and took the keys from the ignition.

I looked at Alison.

"Okay, Joan of Arc," I said. "You want to join the fight in Johannesburg? Get on a 'plane. They leave every day."

I opened the passenger door and leaned in. They looked at me.

"Okay, Missus Blankerscoon, I'll tell you something," I began.

"You've nothing to tell me, Ginley," she snapped back.

"Oh yes I have. I've got this to tell you. All that you did, you shouldn't have done to me. But most of all, you shouldn't have done to anybody."

I stepped back, took my handkerchief from my pocket and threw it into her lap. She opened it and saw the rubber ball, the tubing and the hypodermic. I slammed the door, stepped back, gripped the .38 with both hands, closed my eyes, and fired at the front offside tyre. It made a mess of it. It made the Daimler tilt over. There was a scream from inside the car. Joey came running up. He looked at the damage to the limousine from the alley wall, at the damage to the tyre from the bullet. He shook his head wonderingly.

"Do you know how much these things cost?" he asked, tapping the dented bodywork.

"Go get the fuzz, Joey," I said. He went. There are those occasions on which you have to call the cops.

A sergeant and a constable turned up in a Zephyr. Then four more constables in separate panda cars. I think the busmen must have called those.

The sergeant came across.

"Evenin' all," I tried.

"I know you," he said, "you're a comedian. I caught your act at the Broadway Club."

"Oh yeah?" I said.

"Yeah," he said. "I didn't think much of it."

A distraught Mrs Blankerscoon was being helped from the lopsided Daimler by one of the panda men. I nodded to her.

"Wait till you catch hers," I said.

The sergeant turned to the constable.

"Take this fellow, Fred," he said, "he's a *comedian*."

Never try to be funny with policemen. They're not built for it.

In the Zephyr, I handed the constable the gun.

"Hello, hello, hello," he said, "What's this?" Natch.

About seven the next morning the Zephyr dropped me off in Gambier Terrace. I picked up my lonely little bottle of milk, got out my key, opened the door and went in. I was dog tired as I climbed the three flights to my pad. I'd had three hours sleep in a cell at the main bridewell. I also had a sore throat from talking so much. I must have repeated my story twenty times at least to coppers of various ranks over the preceding twenty-four hours. Still, I was free.

Free till the cops called again, which they threatened to do with alarming frequency until the case or cases came up.

I had had a lot of talking to do to the police. But

172

not as much as William and Ellen and the Blankerscoon dame. The bickering they had started when I got out of the car hardly abated when we all got to the main nick in Hardman Street. That was silly of them, really. Had they shut up, had the dame played the part of the outraged commercial attaché as threatened in the car, she might have come out okay. But she cracked. William tried. He attempted to play it cool and pretend that he didn't know what the fuss was all about. Ellen dissolved into tears and blurted out a self-justification.

Clifford said least. He looked like he wished he had a phial in his tooth he could bite on and get out of it all. And Alison.

Lovely Alison. Student of plasma physics, I found out. So why was she in the Department of Mathematics at the University? I never found that out. Anyway, she coughed up her two cents' worth of the story, helping to vindicate my tale.

The Embassy sent their man down for Mrs Blankerscoon. The coppers didn't like that. They smelt a fix. It looked as though she wasn't going to be sprung. Murder hardly came under the heading of diplomatic immunity, even when you killed one of your own kind. They were all going to be done for murder, murder again, and William for concealing the first murder.

Alison went back to University. She didn't turn up for the trial.

I never saw her again.

I opened the door of the flat and went inside. The light was on. I closed the door and as I did so I heard a familiar voice.

"Cup of tea?" it said. "I heard you coming up the stairs."

Straker was sitting at the table in the kitchen, the pot raised. I nodded. He began to pour.

I went to the table and sat down opposite him.

"All right, I'll marry you," I said.

"I could have been arrested on that train."

"I'd have spoken up for you."

"Where's the money, lad?"

"Down the cop shop."

He put a hand to his head, "Oh dear me," he said, why did you want to go and do a thing like that?" He gave me a hurt look.

"I had to, John. I turned them all in. And the money." I paused, "What are you going to do now?"

"Nothing," he said, shaking his head wearily.

"Aren't you going to get your gun out and lean on me?"

"What gun?" he said, surprised.

"The gun on the tube. You stuck it into me. You had it in your pocket."

"I had no gun," he said. I looked at him incredulously.

"How did you expect to get the money?"

"Threaten you," he said simply.

"With what?"

"Violence of the tongue," he said. I sat back in amazement.

"How come they picked a tough guy like you to snatch the girl?" I asked.

"They didn't. They picked a fellow who fell ill. I... I... er... took his place," he said.

I shook my head in disbelief and we sat there grinning stupidly at each other. Then Straker's face suddenly went grim.

"By God, Eddie. There's some dodgy people about these days," he said.

"What a crummy outfit!" I said. "What a damn crummy, ramshackle outfit they were." I started to laugh.

"Aye," he said, "you're not wrong."

"Gumshoe Ginley and Slyboots Straker. I'm not so hot but you're terrible!"

He looked at me unhappily. "I try, Eddie." He paused. "So you've no money on you, then?"

"Not a bean," I said. I had some of my wages left but I wasn't letting on.

"So you couldn't lend me a couple of quid?"

"A couple of quid? You bum. You absolute Scotch bum. I'm on the dole."

He drained his tea, sighed, stood up and moved to the door. He stopped and turned.

"Would you like to *borrow* a few quid?" he asked eagerly.

I grinned at him, you couldn't help liking him.

"Are you sure you don't want to marry me?" I said.

He grinned back.

"You're a good lad, Eddie."

"You may not think so, if you see the coppers."

"What did I do wrong?" he asked. "Anyway," he added, "I've avoided them before, I can do it again."

"Go on, get out. If the fuzz ask I haven't seen you," I said.

He opened the door. "Gumshoe," he said, shaking his head and smiling.

I raised my teacup to him.

"Here's looking at you, kid," I said.

He went. I closed the door and took down the fedora from the hook behind it. I stuck it on. I crossed to the amplifier and pressed the switch. I got a record out, put it on the deck and dropped the arm on it. I pulled a chair over and sat down facing the speakers. I lit a fag. I tilted the hat over my eyes, lifted my feet on the bed and took a drag from my cigarette.

That was it. The whole schmear finished. The whole hit wrapped up.

"Well, it's one for the money, Two for the show, Three to get ready, Now go cat, go…"

Yeah, sure, I thought. But go where, Elvis? Go where?

CODA

I was acting in an episode of *Parkin's Patch* for Yorkshire Television in Leeds. The director was Michael Apted. Sitting in the canteen, in a powder blue suit, and dripping with gold, was Les Dawson, fidgeting while his wife fetched him a cup of tea. Apted and I took the table next to him, hoping to overhear a few quips.

We were joined by an unshaven chap. He wore tennis shoes, baggy corduroys, a green sloppy joe, and a black jacket, all of which had seen better days. He had a mess of black hair and, like Apted, was handsome.

Very soon he and Apted were drawling away in their posh Oxbridge accents. It was like listening to Trevor Bailey nattering away between overs. Then Apted said, apropos of nothing at all, it seemed to me, "Was it Nietzsche or Wittgenstein who said that the limits of language are the limits of the world?" The unshaven chap said, "No. It was Fatty Arbuckle." I laughed, and that is how I got to know Stephen Frears.

Later, back in London, I talked to him on the

telephone and we discovered that we had a friend in common, Maurice Hatton. I told them both about half an idea I had for a film. I talked about it on and off, for weeks.

Somehow, Maurice had acquired the use of a vicarage in Arundel. He and Stephen locked me in until I had written the first draft of the screenplay. I was only allowed our for food, and to go to the lavatory. Maurice did the cooking, and while I wrote, he and Stephen played football in the back garden. I hated them both.

For the film's release, Collins wanted the 'novelisation'. I dithered and ended up with a week to the deadline. My patient editor, Mary Danby, put me on to Graduate Girls. They would send along someone who would stick with me day and night, typing, as I talked the book.

With two toddlers in a tiny flat, my wife and I had no room for a graduate girl. Stephen, and his wife at the time, Mary-Kay Wilmers, gave me a room in their palatial home in Campden Hill Road, W8.

An Australian arrived who said she had a B.Sc. in Abbo-culture. I chatted about native Australian painting until she typed out, one-fingered, the word 'arboriculture'. On the last day, she looked around at the magnificence of the Frears-Wilmers house and said, "Jeez, I could force myself to live here."

I could force myself to work with Stephen Frears anytime.

Neville Smith
London, 1998

GUMSHOE

THE MOVIE

Director	Stephen Frears
Producer	Michael Medwin
Screenplay	Neville Smith
Cinematographer	Chris Menges

Eddie Ginley	Albert Finney
Ellen	Billie Whitelaw
William	Frank Finlay
Mrs Blankerscoon	Janice Rule
John Straker	Fulton Mackay
Tommy Summers	Bill Dean

Running time	84 minutes

A Memorial Enterprises Production
for Columbia Pictures

Neville Smith won a Writers' Guild Award for his screenplay for the film, *Gumshoe*, which was directed by Stephen Frears and starred Albert Finney and Billie Whitelaw. Smith's recent radio drama adaptation of *The Diary of Samuel Pepys* was also given a Writers' Guild Award. His television work, which includes a number of episodes of the popular drama *The Manageress*, has been broadcast on the BBC, Granada, LWT, Tyne Tees and Channel 4. *Gumshoe* is his only novel.

SLOW DANCER FICTION

Blue Lightning John Harvey (Editor)
ISBN 1 871033 43 8
Gumshoe Neville Smith
ISBN 1 871033 44 6
New Orleans Mourning Julie Smith
ISBN 1 871033 45 4 (UK only)

FORTHCOMING

Ladder of Angels Brian Thompson
ISBN 1 871033 48 9
Solo Hand Bill Moody
ISBN 1 871033 49 7 (UK only)

For further information about Slow Dancer Press
visit our web site
www.mellotone.co.uk
or join our free mailing list.

Slow Dancer Press
59 Parliament Hill London NW3 2TB UK
slowdancer@mellotone.co.uk